THE BRIGADIER'S RUNAWAY BRIDE

DUKES OF WAR #5

⚜

ERICA RIDLEY

Copyright © 2015 Erica Ridley

All rights reserved.

This is a work of fiction. Names, characters, places, and incidents are the product of the author's imagination or are used fictitiously. Any resemblance to actual events, locales, or persons, living or dead, is purely coincidental.

Cover design © Teresa Spreckelmeyer

Model photography: VJ Dunraven, PeriodImages

All rights reserved. Except as permitted under the U.S. Copyright Act of 1976, no part of this publication may be reproduced, distributed, or transmitted in any form or by any means, or stored in a database or retrieval system, without the prior written permission of the author.

ALSO BY ERICA RIDLEY

The *Dukes of War*:
The Viscount's Tempting Minx
The Earl's Defiant Wallflower
The Captain's Bluestocking Mistress
The Major's Faux Fiancée
The Brigadier's Runaway Bride
The Pirate's Tempting Stowaway
The Duke's Accidental Wife
A Match, Unmasked
All I Want

The *Wild Wynchesters*:
The Governess Gambit
The Duke Heist
The Perks of Loving a Wallflower
Nobody's Princess
My Rogue to Ruin

***Heist Club*:**
The Rake Mistake
The Modiste Mishap

***Rogues to Riches*:**
Lord of Chance
Lord of Pleasure
Lord of Night
Lord of Temptation

Lord of Secrets
Lord of Vice
Lord of the Masquerade

The *12 Dukes of Christmas*:
Once Upon a Duke
Kiss of a Duke
Wish Upon a Duke
Never Say Duke
Dukes, Actually
The Duke's Bride
The Duke's Embrace
The Duke's Desire
Dawn With a Duke
One Night With a Duke
Ten Days With a Duke
Forever Your Duke
Making Merry

Gothic Love Stories:
Too Wicked to Kiss
Too Sinful to Deny
Too Tempting to Resist
Too Wanton to Wed
Too Brazen to Bite

Magic & Mayhem:
Kissed by Magic
Must Love Magic
Smitten by Magic

Regency Fairy Tales

Bianca & the Huntsman

Her Princess at Midnight

Missing an Erica Ridley book?

Grab the latest edition of the free, downloadable and printable complete book list by series here:

https://ridley.vip/booklist

ACKNOWLEDGMENTS

As always, I could not have written this book without the invaluable support of my critique partners. Huge thanks go out to Emma Locke and Erica Monroe for their advice and encouragement.

I also want to thank the Historical Romance Book Club on facebook, and my fabulous street team. Your enthusiasm makes the romance happen. Thank you so much!

Four left for war...
Only three made it home.
At first.

CHAPTER 1

March 1816
London, England

Most women would be delighted to find themselves mere moments away from becoming a duchess.

Miss Sarah Fairfax, as it happened, was not most women.

For one, she stood before a temporary altar in a private alcove of the Duke of Ravenwood's London estate with her shoulders back, her chin up, and her belly swollen with child.

For two, Ravenwood—the handsome, eligible duke with whom she was about to wed—was not her unborn child's father.

That had been Edmund Blackpool. The boy whose tousled golden brown locks and dreamy blue eyes had stolen her breath and her heart even when they were children. He was all she'd ever wanted... and would never have. He'd gone off to war three years ago, intending to make the world a better place.

After two years of agonizing separation, last June, she had met him in Bruges, mere days before his company had been sent to Waterloo.

A sharp kick jabbed the wall of Sarah's belly and she smiled to hide a wince of pain. Masking her emotions was all she'd done for the past eight months. Smiling was automatic now. No matter what happened.

Everything traced back to that fateful, impulsive night.

Edmund was no longer plain Mr. Blackpool, but a dashing brigadier with shiny epaulets and matching stars upon his uniform. He was beautiful and passionate and irresistible, and when he'd confessed his wish to marry her if only she'd wait for his return... She was in his arms before he had finished speaking.

He hadn't made it off the battlefield alive.

Next had come the nausea, the dizziness, the desire to do nothing but sleep... and the realization that depression was not the sole cause. She was beyond ruined. She was *pregnant*. Her child would be born a bastard, and live the rest of his life in ostracized infamy, just like his mother.

Sarah faced the vicar and struggled to keep her breaths even, to not betray the weight of the endless pressure of everyone else's expectations. Society. Her peers. Her parents. Herself. She was in this position because she'd *expected* to wed Edmund as soon as he returned from war.

Well, now she knew better than to count on expectations. She was in charge of her own fate now. No, make that two fates. Her knuckle traced the curve of her belly. Their future was up to her.

"Lawrence Pembroke, Duke of Ravenwood," the vicar intoned. "Wilt thou have this woman to be thy wedded wife, to live together after God's ordinance in the holy estate of matrimony? Wilt thou love her, comfort her, honor and keep her in sickness and in health, and forsaking all others, keep thee only unto her, so long as ye both shall live?"

Sarah's throat convulsed. This was a nightmare. She touched her palm to her swollen midsection. Was she really going to go through with this? Would Ravenwood?

"I will," the duke replied before Sarah could interrupt.

If she would have done so.

Her fingers stroked her belly, trying to calm the infant inside. Truth be told, they were moments away from a miracle. The child would be legitimate, not a bastard. Even once Society inevitably did the maths and realized the baby had been conceived long before the ducal wedding, the power of the Ravenwood name would protect them from all but a few whispers.

No one would dare cut them. The baby would be fine.

If the child was a boy, he would inherit a dukedom someday. If the child was a girl, she would be welcomed into Society with open arms. Perhaps marry a duke herself someday. What did it signify if her parents were not in love? If part of Sarah had died on that blood-soaked battlefield alongside her lost lover, did it matter, so long as her child was safe?

The vicar fixed his dark eyes on her. "Miss Sarah Fairfax."

She swallowed. 'Twas a miracle and a nightmare, this union.

Sarah slid the duke a furtive glance. She'd never wished to be a duchess. She'd just wanted Edmund. And now the only way to save her baby's future was to raise his baby as someone else's child. Someone who wasn't doing this for her—or for the baby.

Ravenwood was sacrificing himself at the altar for Edmund. Because for all their lives, they had been the best of friends.

Because Ravenwood hadn't been there that day to save him.

The vicar stared at Sarah. "Wilt thou have this man to be thy wedded husband, to live together after God's ordinance in the holy estate of matrimony? Wilt thou obey him, and serve him, love honor and keep him in sickness and in health, and forsaking all others, keep thee solely unto him, so long as ye both shall live?"

Love him? Forsaking all others? She froze, her lungs suddenly incapable of breath. Her gaze flicked over her shoulder, toward the few souls in attendance.

She hadn't been the only one who had lost Edmund. His twin brother Bartholomew stood at the back of the alcove, his face unreadable. Her stomach twisted. Did he hate her for marrying Ravenwood? For depriving him of a niece or nephew he could claim as his own blood? For being a distraction to Edmund? She turned back to the vicar before her eyes could sting with tears. Crying wouldn't change the past.

The future was her sole concern.

It didn't matter what anyone thought. Not Bartholomew, not her parents, not even the vicar. All that mattered was the baby. She would be the best mother in the history of mothers. There was nothing she wouldn't do to provide for her child. Marrying a man she did not love was the best option.

She set her jaw. As bad as things were, she and the baby were devilish fortunate. Despite so many tragedies—or, perhaps, *because* of them—her child would have a better future than Sarah would ever have dreamed. She would ensure her child never felt unloved or unwanted for a single moment.

Sarah lifted her gaze toward the vicar. "I will."

The vicar nodded. "I require and charge you both, as ye will answer at the dreadful day of judgment when the secrets of all hearts shall be disclosed, that if either of you know any impediment why ye may not be lawfully joined together in matrimony, ye do now confess it."

The alcove was still.

In the ensuing silence, Sarah was suddenly aware of a dozen tiny sounds. The vicar's finger, smoothing a crinkled page. The slight change in Ravenwood's breath, as if he, too, felt the weight of the future upon them. A shuffle in the rear of the alcove as Bartholomew shifted his prosthesis. Or perhaps that movement was the Earl of Carlisle, who had been stone still throughout the entire ceremony.

The earl hadn't just lost a friend. He'd been with them on the battlefield when the twins had been injured. There had scarcely been time to save one of them.

He'd chosen Bartholomew.

Not Edmund. Not the father of her child, the love of her life. The earl had let her betrothed die.

Sarah fixed her gaze on the altar. She could not be angry at Oliver. Or at least, she would not let her bitterness show. He had been faced with a terrible decision, and he'd made the only choice that he could. Edmund had been mortally wounded. His twin was not. Bartholomew was alive because of the earl. Oliver deserved her respect and her sympathy.

He had saved a life. The war was not his fault. The earl had done his best to save everyone he could.

Just like Ravenwood was doing his best to rescue Sarah and her child.

This was her last hope. There was no going back.

The vicar's clear voice echoed through the alcove. "Forasmuch as Lawrence Pembroke, Duke of Ravenwood, and Miss Sarah Fairfax have consented together in holy wedlock, and have witnessed the same before God and this company, and have declared the same by giving and receiving a Ring, and by joining Hands; I pronounce that they are—"

A crash filled the alcove as the well-oiled mahogany doors swung inward and slammed into the walls hard enough to knock the paintings askew.

"*Stop!*" bellowed a deep, familiar voice.

Sarah jerked around in shock and disbelief. The imbalance of her extra weight coupled with her sudden movement sent her careening into the Duke of Ravenwood, who caught her in his arms as a sun-worn gentleman with a scruffy beard and tattered clothing stalked up the aisle.

'Twas her ex-lover, Edmund Blackpool.

Back from the dead.

CHAPTER 2

Three Hours Earlier...

Sarah Fairfax was the sole thought in Edmund Blackpool's mind as he hurried off the rancid passenger ship onto the overcrowded London docks.

She had been the sole thought in his mind from the moment she'd met him in Bruges, during his brief days of leave before heading to Waterloo.

She had been the sole thought in his mind when the bullet had ripped into his chest and he'd collapsed to the trodden ground in a pool of his own blood.

When he awoke a week later amongst an endless row of narrow cots in an austere Flemish convent, his first thought was still Sarah Fairfax.

His second thought was pain.

Oh, God, the pain. His wounds had taken months to heal. The bullet had come from a great enough distance that it cracked two of his ribs when it lodged between them. 'Twas fortunate it hadn't penetrated his lung. In fact, the bullet was the least of his concerns. He and many others had apparently been trampled in the ensuing melee. Every limb was splinted, every inch of skin mottled with contusions. Just lying there breathing caused more agony than he'd have imagined possible.

And so he'd thought of Sarah.

Dark brown hair the deep hue of fine chocolate. Wide brown eyes, gazing up at him from beneath long dark lashes. Rosy lips, rosy cheeks, a waist he could nearly span with his fingers. She was a perfect pixie, bewitching him with her porcelain skin and teasing smiles from hundreds of miles away.

Back in London at last, Edmund pushed through the crowded dock and made his way to the street. He had no baggage to slow him down. No coin with which to hail a hack. He would make his way to Mayfair the same way he'd traveled across Flanders to the coast: on foot.

His fraying boots would fall apart before he did. His slowly mended bones might be weaker, but Edmund was stronger than ever. His feet, and his determination, could take him anywhere.

The question was *where*.

His first impulse was to go straight to Sarah. He hadn't seen her in eight months, two weeks, and five days. Not since promising to wed her the moment he returned from the war.

Well, he was back. He was also wearing the same clothes he'd left Belgium in. He'd washed up as often as he could aboard the freezing ship, but a comb would be more than welcome. His chin hadn't seen a razor for a month. He couldn't recall a single time that Sarah had ever turned away from him in disgust, and he certainly didn't wish for her to see him like this.

Which left what? His rented townhouse was no

doubt long gone, and there was no time to waste on fabric and a tailor. He was, however, possessed of one asset most gentlemen could not boast.

An identical twin.

He hunched forward into the bitter wind and told himself the sudden chill had nothing to do with his fears for his brother.

Eight and a half months since he'd seen his twin. If Bartholomew was still alive—of *course* Bartholomew would still be alive!—his clothes would be a perfect fit. His valet would have Edmund dandified within an inch of his life in a matter of minutes. He could be off to woo Sarah in less time than it took to boil a kettle.

Of course, if Bartholomew was still alive, that would also mean he'd done the one thing he'd sworn never to do. It would mean Bartholomew had abandoned his twin right when Edmund needed him most.

And then left him for dead.

An insidious thought. An *impossible* thought. Edmund flung the idea away like so much rubbish. His twin would never consign him to such a fate.

Which left what? If Bartholomew hadn't made it off the battlefield alive… If he'd been captured by the French, or trampled into jelly by the fleeing horses…

Edmund walked faster. In eight long months, he still hadn't managed to reconcile his hurt and fury at being left to die with his abject terror that perhaps it hadn't been by choice. Both possibilities were awful. Soon, he would arrive at his brother's townhouse and find out the truth, one way or another. Soon, he would be back in Sarah's arms.

Sarah would never leave him. Of this, Edmund was certain. She had been his constant shadow since they were old enough to roll down hills together, between their parents' adjoining country estates in Kent. Her affections had never wavered.

His hands went clammy despite the winter chill. What if she was not in London, but in Kent? What if he were still weeks away from seeing her again?

He couldn't bear to be apart another moment. He already regretted the lost years of his youth, when he'd thought catching bugs and kicking balls—and, later, boxing and carousing—were more important endeavors than spending time with a girl he could see anytime he wished.

Until he couldn't.

If he had but known that night in Bruges would be the last time he'd see her, he would have... Oh, who was he fooling? He would have done nothing different. He'd wanted to marry her then, and he wanted to marry her now. He'd *desired* her then, and he desired her now. If he could change anything at all, it would be to have held her in his arms a few moments longer.

This time, he would never let her go.

Edmund ignored his blistered feet and increased his pace. By the time he reached his brother's crescent row of terraced houses, snow swirled down from the sooty gray sky, blurring the air. He blew on his chapped fingers to warm them enough to uncurl, then gave the knocker a hefty bang.

His heart stuttered when the door swung open to reveal his twin's stoic butler. Relief flooded through him. If Crabtree still ruled the roost, Bartholomew must have survived! It took all Edmund's restraint not to elbow past the butler and dash into the townhouse to find his brother.

Crabtree's jaw dropped. "Master *Blackpool?*"

"In the flesh." Edmund's body shook, he was so giddy to be among familiar faces at last. It had been so long since anyone had so much as recognized him. He'd almost forgotten the simple pleasure of seeing, and being seen. Of being anyone at all, other than a nameless, voiceless nothing lost in a foreign land.

He was finally home at last. Life would not only return to normal; life would *return*. His family, his friends, his secret fiancée... Even his brother's imperturbable butler was a sight for sore eyes. Edmund had never seen Crabtree so much as blink in surprise, and here the man was, gaping in astonishment. Edmund pressed his lips together. He could hardly wait to see his twin's reaction!

"Is my brother at home?" he asked, trying to hide his grin.

Before Crabtree could respond, a tall thin man with tightly curled locks skidded into the entryway squealing, "*Mas*ter *Black*pool!" at a pitch high enough to break glass.

Edmund's lips quirked at his brother's valet. "Wonderful to see you, Fitz, old man. I trust you haven't allowed my twin to gad about in Society looking anything less than his best? Reflects badly on me, you know, what with everyone mixing us up all the time."

The valet spluttered speechlessly, his eyes bulging so wide as to be comical. "I—He—You..."

Edmund's elation began to dim. "I say, as lovely as it is to chat, would one of you mind terribly running to fetch my brother? I haven't seen him in eight months, and I'd really like..." His voice trailed off as a familiar looking young woman with red-gold hair and a shocked expression rushed into the entryway. He blinked in surprise. "Daphne?"

Her eyes widened in disbelief. "*Edmund?*"

He tried to reconcile the girl he hadn't seen since his youth with the elegant young lady now standing before him. In the entryway to his brother's townhouse. Along with the butler and the valet. "Daphne, what are you doing here?"

"What are *you* doing here?" She ran to him and threw her arms around him and embraced him as if they were family. "I can't believe you're alive!"

He patted her on the shoulder awkwardly. He hadn't been embraced in eight long months, and he'd rather hoped his twin would be the first to earn the distinction. "Where's my brother?"

Still hugging him, Daphne's voice was muffled by the ragged shirt covering Edmund's chest. "At the Duke of Ravenwood's wedding."

Edmund grinned despite himself. Finicky Ravenwood, married? Edmund had doubted that day would ever come, and was truly pleased to find it had. "Ravenwood finally found his love match? I cannot wait to meet the debutante charming enough to ensnare His Grace's romantic heart."

Daphne's fingers dug into Edmund's arms as she jerked her pale countenance away from his chest.

"No," she gasped. "It's much worse than that. Edmund, the duke is going to marry *Sarah*."

Edmund's stomach dropped. He shook off Daphne's fingers. "*My* Sarah?"

Daphne nodded. "She's—"

"Where?" he barked.

"At Ravenwood House. Right now."

"Over my dead body." Edmund snapped around and marched down the front steps. There was no time to spare for starched cravats and polished boots. He had to stop a wedding.

"Where is your carriage?" Daphne called after him. "Do you mean to summon a hack?"

Damn it. Edmund's fists tightened at his powerlessness. In the long months it had taken to finally return home, he had never felt his lack of coin as keenly as he did right now.

"I arrived on foot," he admitted through clenched teeth. He would *not* let that prevent him from stopping the wedding. "If I hurry—"

"You'll never get there in time." Daphne's face brightened. "Bartholomew left in his curricle. You can take the landau."

"Too slow." Edmund shot a glance over his shoulder at the waning sunlight. "I'll get there faster if you just loan me a horse."

"Done." She turned toward the butler. "Crabtree?"

The butler had resumed his hallmark bored expression. "Already sent a footman to the stables, ma'am."

Horse hooves clopped against the cobblestone road as a stableboy raced a black stallion straight toward them.

Edmund's blood raced. The moment the stableboy slid onto the ground, Edmund launched himself up and into the saddle.

"Wait!" Daphne called out, her voice urgent. "You should know *why* Sarah is marrying the duke. She—"

"She's *not* marrying him," Edmund shouted back as he pointed the stallion toward Ravenwood House. "She's marrying *me*."

CHAPTER 3

*E*dmund flew across the cobblestone streets as fast as the stallion could carry him. Sweat raced down his back despite the bitter March wind. Devil take it. If he was too late… If the woman who'd haunted his dreams ended up someone else's wife…

He lowered his head against the wind and urged the stallion as fast as he dared. 'Twas wretched out. The streets were slippery with icy pockets of snow. Teeming with carriages and pedestrians. The stench of horse manure and dirt. Edmund hated it all. The clamor, the crowds, the chaos. London was repellant.

It was too much like war. Like being lost. Like the endless nightmares of chasing after his brother, running toward the other soldiers, and always being left behind. He'd woken in cold sweats then. No wonder he was reliving it now.

But a wedding was underway, and he had to stop it.

Sarah was the one bright light in the darkness of his world. Pure and sweet and beautiful, she was everything he desired. Everything he'd longed for all those lonely nights. The heat of her skin. The scent of her hair. The feel of her body as he lifted her slender form above him and—

Ravenwood House rose against the blinding sunset like a dragon unfurling its wings. It was not a small part of a crescent of row houses. Its three floors and two annexes *were* the crescent.

Edmund's jaw tightened. The stallion reared at the sight as if it, too, sensed danger lurking within those elegant walls.

There were no longer pedestrians crowding the pristine road. No life of any kind. Any visiting carriages had already been tucked out of sight inside the mews. And of course, nothing so gauche as a hired hackney dared sit idle before the grand ducal estate.

Tough. Edmund tucked his head and raced his horse right over the manicured grass of the front lawn. If Ravenwood's perfect garden got mussed, so be it. There was no time to waste.

As Edmund neared the front door, servants streamed out of the estate in alarm. He leapt from the stallion and tossed the reins to the closest gaping footman before shouldering his way inside the mansion.

Of course the servants wouldn't invite him to enter. He hadn't been to Ravenwood House since he'd purchased his commission four years ago, so the staff was unlikely to recognize him.

He also knew he looked a fright. Tattered, mismatched clothing. Scarred face covered by a five-week beard. A scowl fierce enough to terrify the devil himself—and with good reason. If Edmund was too late to stop the ceremony…

"Where's the wedding?" he snarled to the housemaids.

One of them keeled into the others in a dead faint.

A male voice broke in. "Sir, I'm afraid you'll have to…"

Edmund whirled to face Ravenwood's butler, whose jaw dropped with the shock of recognition. "Master Blackpool?"

"Where are they?" Edmund demanded, his voice hoarse. "I have to stop the wedding."

"Master Blackpool, it is splendid to see you alive and… well, alive, sir, but I cannot in good conscience allow you to thwart His Grace's wishes, particularly on this day of—"

"The alcove of the back parlor," gasped one of the maids. "The blue one, next to the billiards room."

"*Agnes.*" One of the other servants grabbed the maid's arm. "You'll be sacked for this!"

"But it's all so romantic…"

Edmund missed whatever else was said because he was already tearing down the corridor toward the rear of the mansion.

He hadn't forgotten the way. As a young man, he, his twin brother, and their three best friends—Xavier Grey, Oliver York, and the Duke of Ravenwood—had spent many a lazy evening drinking the duke's port and battling for temporary dominance over the billiards table. It had all seemed terribly important and worldly when Edmund was but a young buck of seventeen years.

He was now six-and-twenty and this particular battle for dominance would determine the fate of the rest of his life.

His breath quickened. On the ride over, he hadn't let himself think of anything except getting back to Sarah. No good would come of wondering how she'd wound up in the arms of Edmund's (better looking, better moneyed, better mannered) lifelong friend. It didn't matter. She was *his*.

The fact that Edmund's own brother had apparently come along to witness the unholy event also did not bear contemplating. There was no room in Edmund's atrophied heart to feel betrayed or wounded, when he was so bloody thrilled to discover his brother was even alive. The rest would come later. He and Bartholomew were *twins*. The best of friends. Inseparable and indistinguishable. Edmund had dreamed of being reunited with his brother almost as often as he'd dreamed of being reunited with Sarah.

And he would not let the Duke of Ravenwood stop him.

Edmund flung open the parlor door and charged forward bellowing, *"Stop!"* as he raced up the makeshift aisle.

The first thing he saw was her hair. Thick and chestnut and familiar, the long tresses had been gathered up in a shiny mass and pinned to the back of her head, just as it had been in Bruges. She was his siren. He could already smell her soap and feel the softness of her dark brown curls as he plucked the pins free one by one.

As if responding to the force of his thoughts, the power of his love, Sarah turned to face him.

Edmund pulled up short. His stomach dropped, his jaw dropped, his bloody *heart* dropped because Sarah was... pregnant.

Not just pregnant: *hugely* pregnant. His slender, innocent, doe-eyed bride had doubled in size since last he'd seen her. His stomach dropped. No wonder there was a wedding.

He cut a furious glance toward Ravenwood, who held up his palms and shook his head.

The vicar clutched the cross hanging from his neck and backed away.

"Not Ravenwood," Sarah said, her voice cracking. "The baby is yours."

Edmund's ears roared. If anyone was speaking, he could not hear them. Sarah was pregnant. The baby was *his*. Sarah was pregnant. He was going to be a *father*. Sarah was right there in front of him, waiting for his reaction with tears in her eyes.

Edmund's position had not changed. His will had only been reinforced.

"Stop the wedding." He marched forward, his gaze locked on hers. "She marries *me*."

Ravenwood sidestepped in front of Sarah, blocking Edmund's view of his bride.

Edmund's eyes narrowed.

Ravenwood turned his back on Edmund to curl his insolent fingers gently about Sarah's trembling shoulders. "You don't have to marry me, Sarah," he told her in his calm, quiet voice. "But you don't have to marry Blackpool, either."

Edmund's fingers flexed into fists. If the duke had a death wish, so be it.

"I have never had a choice," said Sarah, her expression haunted. "Women have never had choices. Not really. Least of all someone in my position."

"Because of the baby?" Ravenwood's voice lowered. "I told you I would have no problem raising your child as my own, and affording him or her all the benefits of—"

"Your wedding is *off*." Edmund shoved the duke aside to take Sarah's hands. She had loved him before. She would love him again.

He lifted her swollen fingers to his lips to kiss them, but stopped when he remembered the unkempt beard protruding from his face. He would not kiss her like this. Not even her fingers. Not when she'd been about to wed a duke who would have showered her with money and estates and thousands of ducal advantages that Edmund could never replicate.

He let her fingers drop. "We'll call the banns tomorrow."

The vicar cleared his throat. "Tomorrow is Monday—"

"It doesn't matter," Sarah interrupted. "I can't wait for banns." She cast a pointed look toward her round belly. "*We* can't wait for banns."

No wonder she was in a hurry. Edmund swallowed. He still couldn't fathom it.

He'd spent so many months just trying to get through one more day, one more hour, that he hadn't given any thought to the future at all. Still wasn't certain he had one. Things like futures could vanish in the blink of an eye.

All he'd wanted was Sarah, if only for one more night. One more moment.

Well, here she was. Standing right before him. With a chasm the size of the world between them.

His stomach churned. What had happened between her and Ravenwood? The duke was bloody *nice* enough to do something foolish and romantic like wed his missing friend's bride so the babe would not be born illegitimate. The duke was also *rich* enough to have sent out a hunting party or two in search of said missing friend. Hell, the duke's know-all older sister could probably have rescued Edmund on her own in a matter of hours, and cleaned up the French/Austrian political climate that same day after tea.

Edmund would've settled for just being found.

"Well, you're not marrying *him*," he said flatly,

without sparing Ravenwood so much as a glance. "So you're right. You have no choice."

"Be reasonable," began the duke. "You haven't—"

Edmund cut him off with a chilling glance. "This is *my* baby and *my* bride. You might notice that I've just returned from war. A wise man wouldn't speak to me right now, for fear of how I might react."

"Of course I'll marry you, Edmund." Sarah flashed him a wobbly smile, her eyes glistening. "I've never wanted anything else."

His chest thudded in pleasure. He longed to reach for her. But not like this. Not covered in dust and dressed in rags. She deserved so much more. He would prove he was a man she could be proud of.

"Brother..." came a voice from somewhere behind him.

Heart thundering, Edmund whirled toward the rear of the alcove. *Bartholomew*. Edmund's chest tightened with love at the ridiculous sight of him. Bartholomew's valet had trussed his master up just as beautifully and ostentatiously as Edmund remembered.

Which only made him feel less worthy of Sarah's love.

Where Edmund was covered with grime and too much facial hair, Bartholomew was starched and tailored and shaved into perfection. Where Edmund's skin was unfashionably brown, Bartholomew's was properly porcelain. Where Edmund's borrowed boots had begun to separate at the soles, Bartholomew... now bore a false limb?

Edmund's shocked gaze flew up to meet his brother's. Were it not for the telltale clapping sound as the wooden prosthetic snapped into place with each step, neither Bartholomew's manner nor appearance would have given any hint that one of the most celebrated dandies in London was missing half of one his legs. Edmund's heart clenched.

This, at least, indicated why *Bartholomew* had not led the search party for his missing twin. He would not have been able to walk for many months. Perhaps had even spent time recovering in hospitals himself. His injury explained so much.

Edmund swallowed. He hated himself for being relieved that there was a reason his brother had not come to find him. Never would Edmund wish the slightest harm on his twin, much less the loss of a leg. But, well… when one returned from war to discover one's bride about to wed one's childhood friend, one could easily begin to think he'd been forgotten completely.

Bartholomew opened his arms.

Edmund swallowed his brother in an embrace fierce enough to make up for several of their lost months.

"I hope I'm crushing your hideous cravat beyond all salvation," he whispered into his brother's ear.

"I hope the French haven't permanently turned you off from bathing," his twin shot back.

A bark of laughter escaped from Edmund's throat. He clapped his brother on the back and broke their embrace to get a better look at him. "What happened to you?"

"I decided to be an Original. Any dandy can have *two* feet," Bartholomew returned with a careless wave of his hand. He stared at Edmund as if he couldn't quite credit that he was actually home. "I've missed you so much. What happened to *you?*"

Edmund's smile fell and his mind shuttered closed. He didn't wish to discuss what had happened to him. He had finally learned that the only way to stop dwelling on the past was to stop thinking about it altogether. To concentrate on the moment. On right now.

And right now, he had a bride to talk back to the altar. "Don't suppose you'd loan me the use of your valet, brother?"

CHAPTER 4

When Sarah arrived back home at her parents' London townhouse, her mother was on her knees peering beneath the dining room buffet table and her father was in his study packing books into boxes.

Not the housekeeper. Not the footmen. Her *parents*. Because they didn't have servants anymore, save for an underpaid maid-of-all-work who they were unlikely to be able to retain.

The Fairfax pockets weren't simply to let. They'd passed that milestone ages ago, and spiraled down into unsurmountable debt. Again.

Sarah had never told a soul about her family's struggles. She was too ashamed.

Soon, however, there would be no hiding it. The Fairfaxes' London days were over. No more modistes, no more soirees, no more nights at the theater. Ever since she was a small child, having a permanent home in London had been her dream. Her life thus far had boasted very little permanence. She never seemed to know from one day to the next what the future might bring.

The Fairfaxes would be returning to their country

cottage forthwith, and they'd be fortunate indeed if they got to keep it. The books Sarah's father packed so lovingly—the books given to him by his father, and his grandfather before him—were not earmarked for their country cottage, but rather a private collector. They were to be sold, along with all the other Fairfax valuables, in order to settle their overdue rent and pay for passage back to Kent for the entire family.

The situation was not entirely Sarah's fault. Her mother had never displayed the slightest interest in whether there was a limit to their modest finances, and Sarah's father had never displayed the slightest interest in anything other than indulging his wife.

Love matches like that could only lead to ruin.

This was not the first time that the Fairfax family's circumstances had been reduced dramatically. The first such incident (that Sarah was old enough to remember) had occurred when she was but ten years old. Her dolls had been sold. Her music instructor sacked. Her faded dresses became increasingly ill-fitting. In short, it was the end of the world as far as ten-year-old Sarah was concerned.

Until she'd met Edmund. Beautiful, wonderful, lovable Edmund.

Her parents' new cottage was modest at best, but it was also on a parcel of land bordering the Blackpool estate.

The Blackpools were not rich—especially when compared to the titled neighbors who also held property nearby—but to Sarah, the handsome Blackpool twins were a welcome escape from the doldrums of impoverished youth.

It began with running and fishing and rolling down hills whilst shrieking with laughter. Normal things. Little-girl things. Until her parents overspent their funds *again* and even their cramped little cottage was in danger of being ripped from them.

That was the first time her older brother Anthony came home with tear-stained cheeks and a black eye. He had gambled. And lost more than he'd arrived with. The proprietor of the back-door gaming den was displeased, but Anthony had scarcely been fourteen years old. His failure was preordained. The proprietor had allowed the boy in with every intention of fleecing him.

The gambit succeeded. Once. But Sarah's brother was not so easily discouraged.

To this day, she did not know where Anthony procured enough coin to gamble with, but within a fortnight he had come home with enough blunt to keep the roof over their heads for another six months. Her parents were relieved. Anthony was thrilled. He had not only provided for his family, he'd found the answer to never being poor again: gambling.

Sarah, on the other hand, had found a different solution to the problem. Marriage to Edmund Blackpool, the boy she adored.

If only he would have her.

Her family was undistinguished. An embarrassment, even. They told her the best she could hope for was someone young and pleasant, who was neither on the hunt for a title or an heiress, because he didn't need one. Someone who wasn't rich enough to have pretensions of marrying up, but who had enough financial stability to be reasonably comfortable for the rest of his life.

She didn't want the "best she could hope for." She wanted Edmund.

He was handsome and adventurous. Fearless and exciting. Reckless and romantic. He rubbed shoulders with aristocrats and yet still had time to take a maturing young girl for sunset walks along the winding river. He stole her first kiss. And then he stole her heart.

Sarah spread her hands over her belly and sighed.

What had started out as a girlish infatuation had turned into something more. Something desperately real. Something hopeless. When Edmund had bought his commission and sailed off to war, she had been convinced her life was over. All was lost without him. Their future was everything.

Of *course* she wrote him love letters with every scrap of parchment she could find. Of *course* she took the first passenger boat to Bruges when Edmund wrote to say he would have a short leave and he'd like to spend it with her.

Of *course* a single night's indiscretion had left her lover gone and left Sarah eight months pregnant.

The front door banged open and her brother Anthony burst inside, all sparkling green eyes and matching dimples beneath a snow-lined hat cocked at a rakish angle.

"Who wants to stay in this hovel at least six more months?" he called out, his self-satisfied grin giving his handsome face an irresistible charm.

Sarah's mother pushed herself up off the floor and threw her arms about her son's neck. "Oh, Anthony," she cried happily. "I knew you could do it!"

Sarah's father grunted, but did not cease stacking books into boxes. The buyer's offer had been generous, but only on the condition that the deal was final. Documents had been signed. The Fairfaxes might stay in the townhouse a few months longer, but their cherished library now had a new home.

Anthony let go of their mother and swept Sarah into his arms. "And how is my favorite duchess, eh?

Shouldn't you be... oh, I don't know. Off duchessing?"

The townhouse became preternaturally silent.

Frowning, Anthony released Sarah. "What happened?"

"She didn't do it," her father ground out, as if he took this act as a personal slight. He likely did.

Anthony laughed in disbelief. "Never say you jilted Ravenwood!"

"Not exactly." Sarah clutched her fingers to her chest. She still couldn't believe the miracle. "The situation—"

"Edmund Blackpool is back," her mother interrupted with a scowl. "That's why she didn't do it."

"But that's wonderful!" Anthony kissed both of Sarah's cheeks before pulling her into another laughing embrace. "I thought Blackpool was dead. We all thought he was! What happened? When did he get home? *How* did he get home? Is this the happiest day of your life? You got to jilt a duke *and* get the love of your life back. You must be the luckiest woman in the world!"

Sarah's answering smile trembled. It *was* the happiest day of her life. Not for jilting Ravenwood—the duke had surprised her by being her best and staunchest supporter since the day she'd confessed her secret. He certainly did not deserve ridicule for being the kindest man of her acquaintance, or sacrificing himself to save someone as lowly as her.

He no longer had to. Edmund was back.

Improbably, wonderfully, terribly. His return was everything she'd wanted since the moment she discovered she was increasing. But her prayers had been answered a little too late. Her dreams of a life in London with her baby and her husband were as substantial as smoke. The child would be born before the banns could be read, and would be forever labeled a bastard. None of them would ever be accepted in Polite Society again.

She could have circumvented all that by marrying Ravenwood after all... But for her, there had never been anyone but Edmund.

Until now.

She curved her hands over her belly and smiled when the baby inside rewarded her with a sharp kick.

It no longer mattered what Sarah wanted, what she had dreamed. The only thing that mattered was the baby. Ensuring the infant's future was the best future Sarah could possibly provide. She was a mother now, and that's what mothers did.

Correction: what *good* mothers did.

Sarah sighed. Clearly she had inherited more than a small bit of her mother's flightiness, because from the second Edmund burst into the ceremony, she'd no longer wanted to be a duchess.

She just wanted Edmund.

Seeing his face had been like being flooded with magic. He was sunshine and sultry nights. Laughter and sensuous kisses. The other half of her heart.

For months, she'd longed for the dashing, carefree young man who was always happy to chase butterflies or swim in the river or spend lazy afternoons on their backs in the grass to look for pictures in the clouds. The Edmund who'd responded to her love letters with a fervor to match her own. The Edmund who had nicked her garter ribbon as if it were a maiden's medieval token bestowed upon her knight, and promised to bring her a ring as soon as he returned home from war.

But the man who'd returned was a stranger. No ring. No smiles. No love words, or even a simple kiss. He'd come back... but he hadn't come back *Edmund*.

"I don't know where he's been," she said dully. "He won't talk to me. He just demanded that we wed posthaste and then left me. Again."

Anthony frowned. He dragged her into the furthest corner of the sitting room and lowered his voice. "Do you still have the blunt I gave you?"

Sarah nodded guiltily. It wasn't enough money to ensure independence, but it would have covered several months' rent for her parents' London townhouse. If she had been a good daughter, she could have offered it to them before they'd had to resort to selling the family library.

If she'd been a good daughter, she wouldn't have gotten pregnant and turned her life upside down.

Well, now she had new priorities. That money was for emergencies. A few months' security, should something financially terrible happen. Something like: not being a duchess after all. Something like: the love of her life returns, and their relationship disintegrates because they can't keep food on the table. She shivered. Money might not solve everything, but poverty was a dark tunnel into Hell.

Had she finally got Edmund back only to be dropped into a new nightmare?

"Those funds are yours." Anthony squeezed her hand, keeping his voice low. "Don't you dare give that money to our parents."

She nodded, but her throat tightened with worry. Would it be enough?

Her brother had opened an account for her the very day she told him about the baby. Every time he won at the gaming tables, he brought a portion to their father and deposited another sum in her secret account. Her brother loved her. He wanted to save her.

He'd given her enough money to escape into the

countryside, have the baby someplace no one knew her name, give the child up to an orphanage, and return home as if nothing had happened.

Sarah could think of nothing more horrid. The child was *hers*. Hers and Edmund's. Come what may.

"What am I to do?" She laid her forehead on her brother's shoulder. "Where are Edmund and I to live? *How* are we to live? If you could have seen him, Anthony. He didn't look like Edmund. He looked like—like a street beggar." She swallowed hard, hating that poverty terrified her. Hated what it meant for her future, for her marriage, for her baby. "He clearly has nothing. No clothes. No home." She stared up at her brother in desperation. "Am I to be poor again? To raise my child as we were raised—never knowing if tomorrow's meal would come from footmen or from animal troughs?"

"*Never.*" Her brother's green eyes flashed with determination and reckless zeal. "I'll win you more pin money than a person could ever spend. Just you see. We will never again lie awake hungry, I swear it."

"Anthony, *wait—*"

But her brother was already gone, flying out the front door just as quickly as he'd blown in.

Tears of frustration stung Sarah's eyes. She rubbed her temples to try and ease the pounding in her head. Perhaps Anthony would return home in a matter of hours, flush with pride and success. Or perhaps the next she saw him, he would lie coughing in a wretched cell in debtor's gaol for betting—and losing—more than he could afford.

Again.

She eased down onto the worn sofa and set her jaw. No more feeling sorry for herself. Not now, not ever. Her sole concern was making the best possible future for the baby.

Oh, God. A *baby*. Would she ever be ready for such responsibility?

The back of her head slumped against the sofa as she closed her eyes and ran a hand over her belly. It would happen soon. Terrifyingly soon. Instead of just being Sarah, she would be Sarah and Baby.

And Edmund.

Joy washed over her at the thought. He was back home. Home and alive! She smiled with her eyes still closed, hugging herself with happiness. She could scarcely credit it. 'Twas a true miracle.

But if *she* had been unprepared to be a mother... What about Edmund? He was back from the dead, and *this* was what awaited him?

She had changed just as much as he had. Her body was distorted and ungainly. It would take more than a maid and a bit of soap to make her look like the girl he'd proposed to, the girl he thought he'd come home to. She wasn't that girl any longer. Could never be her again. She was a mother now, with the bulging belly and swollen feet to prove it. She sighed.

At least she'd finally stopped vomiting in the mornings.

Her lips curved. That would've been all the ceremony would have needed. She could've jilted the Duke of Ravenwood and then cast up her accounts all over his cravat. She was already infamous. Why not *ensure* she was never invited back?

She opened her tired eyes and stared up at the cracked ceiling. Everything was unraveling faster than she could stitch it back together. What she needed most was the one thing she couldn't have: time. Time to reacquaint with Edmund and reinforce their love. Time for him to rejoin normal life before having fatherhood thrust upon him. Time to figure out what on earth she was going to do with a baby.

Perhaps the Duke of Ravenwood could gift them a small sum to keep poverty at bay. She drew a shaky breath. Most people had too much pride to accept the charity of others. Sarah had none. Edmund, on the other hand, would want to solve things himself. He wasn't even speaking to Ravenwood. There was no chance of Edmund begging for help or handouts. It might be years before the two men could be friends again. If friendship were still possible.

A knock sounded upon the front door, followed immediately by the creak of its hinges.

Sarah shook her head. Her brother had left with such haste, he hadn't bothered to secure the door. Whoever was outside was already halfway in.

She pushed heavily to her feet and waddled over to greet the caller. No one else was likely to. Her father wasn't packing his books simply because there were no footmen to do so—he didn't trust non-Fairfax hands with the family heirlooms. Likewise, her mother wouldn't hesitate to drop to the floor to ensure no stray coin or jewel was being left behind— but "maid" and "butler" were not among her duties.

The sole maid-of-all-work they still did have was little more than an exhausted child, and was currently out behind the townhouse, cleaning the chamber pots.

Which left Sarah to start the kettle a-boil or heave logs onto the waning fire or leap up to answer doors.

As much as one could leap whilst enormously pregnant. Inglorious at best.

Out duchessing, her brother had said. Sarah's feet slowed. What would that have been like?

She reached around her belly and pushed the door the rest of the way open. Her breath caught.

Edmund stood there.

Not the dirty, unkempt street-beggar Edmund

who had disrupted her clandestine wedding. Her heart raced. The old Edmund. The *real* Edmund.

The white flash of his teeth in his slow, familiar smile nearly brought her to her knees.

His thick brown hair had been trimmed and coiffed into the mirror image of his fashionable brother's. The beard was gone, leaving Edmund's chiseled jaw smooth and eminently touchable. His sun-browned skin was still unfashionably dark, but the bronze tone only made his white teeth and crystalline blue eyes that much more arresting. As to the rest of him…

His shoulders were as wide as she remembered. His body was more lean, but just as strong and powerful. Perhaps more so. His cravat was perfectly starched and perfectly white, contrasting beautifully with the dark blue of his coat and the supple leather of the buckskin breeches covering his muscled thighs.

Gone were the ill-fitting shoes with the soles barely attached. His feet and calves were now encased in shiny black Hessians. There was no longer any trace of whatever he'd been through en route to the wedding. He even smelled like London—new leather, expensive soap, imported perfume.

He held out a bouquet of flowers. Not roses or lilies, as a debutante being courted might expect, but a simple clutch of the gorgeous red poppies she'd admired lining the streets during their stolen moments in Bruges.

She brought them to her nose and breathed in deeply, allowing the memories of the past to envelop her. She had been so much younger eight short months ago. So feckless and foolhardy. So madly in love. Just as she was now.

"I wish to apologize." Edmund's low, deep voice

washed over her with the same aching familiarity as his big strong hands, his soft wide lips. "I am not apologizing for stopping the ceremony. But I do regret causing you embarrassment and discomfort. That was never my intention."

She lowered the flowers and stepped back from the open doorway, her head spinning at the sight of him. Just as it had done when he'd interrupted the wedding. "Come in."

As he stepped inside, his presence seemed to fill the entire townhouse.

Her blood raced. She could not think. She could barely breathe. Not with him so close after all this time. Her heart pounded. She needed to sit down before the dizziness overtook her.

"You are mine," he said urgently. "Just as I am yours. We promised ourselves to each other, and I mean to keep that promise."

Trembling, she led him to the sofa and eased onto one of the worn cushions. Her fingers touched her protruding belly. "I haven't forgotten a single moment."

His wry smile didn't reach his eyes. "Of course you haven't."

She couldn't look away from the piercing blue of his gaze. Eight months ago, they were lovers. Naked, needy, devouring each other with hungry kisses as his hard member thrust within her.

Today they were strangers.

"What happened?" she asked. She sensed, rather than saw, the violent wave of anger roll through him.

He collected himself just as quickly and spoke with deliberate calm. "The banns must be read on three consecutive Sundays. The first reading will be a week from—"

"There's not enough time. We have only a fortnight. The babe will be born a bastard."

"The infant will be our *child*." His jaw clenched. "I will not let him be born illegitimate. I have applied for a special license."

Sarah glanced away. She understood the reality of their situation. Edmund was beautiful to look at, but he was neither rich nor titled nor influential. A mere Mister would not be granted a special license. They would be wed by banns. Their child would be a bastard. There was nothing to be done.

"Shall we live here?" She picked at her morning dress. "With my parents?"

Of course they would not. They could not. The lease was precarious at best. Nor was there anywhere else to go. The Fairfax cottage in Kent was even smaller. There was no room for baby, much less a baby and a husband. She was simply pointing out what they would not be able to offer the child: a home.

Edmund shook his head. "As you may have surmised, I came here as quickly as I could. I paused only to make myself presentable, and did not spare a moment even to speak with my brother. But his townhouse—"

"—is not large enough to hold us."

He frowned. "Have you seen his property?"

"I don't have to. Bartholomew was a bachelor. You cannot convince me his townhouse contains guest quarters and a nursery. Although I suppose that will have to change."

Edmund's eyes widened and his shoulders began to shake.

Alarmed, Sarah twisted to face him fully. "What is it?"

"Of course." He laughed, but as before, his eyes

did not laugh with him. "She was gone when I returned to the townhouse, and in the turmoil of stopping the wedding and discovering you with child, I had completely forgotten her presence earlier…" His tone was empty. "Bartholomew married little Daphne Vaughan, did he?"

Sarah's throat tightened. What a wretched way to find out one's twin had moved on without him. She touched his knee. "A week ago. They came back to Town because of the wedding. Neither Ravenwood nor I were willing to wed without Bartholomew's…"

"Without my brother's blessing," Edmund finished bitterly when she failed to complete the thought. "Charming."

"We thought you were *dead*," she burst out, grasping his forearm with her hand. "I've been in mourning for the past eight months… Bartholomew has been in mourning for the past eight months… Ravenwood didn't take off his armband until the vicar arrived to take our vows. No one forgot you, Edmund. We thought you were gone forever."

"I suppose you're delighted that I'm back. No more dreary dukedom. No more extravagant London estate, no worries about making do in a far more luxurious mansion cresting the best hill in the entire Kent countryside." Edmund stretched out his legs and propped his head back against his hands. "I imagine every Ravenwood property has an entire wing of nurseries at one's disposal."

"I am beyond delighted to have you back. I prayed for your safe return every single night. If I'd had the slightest idea you might still be alive, I would never have stood before the altar with Ravenwood. Please try to understand. We did what we did because of the baby. She is the greatest innocent in all of this." Sarah placed a protective palm against her belly and glared at Edmund. "I would do anything to keep her safe. I would give my life to make hers better. I would wed the devil himself."

"And so you shall." His gaze bore into hers. "You're mine, Sarah. I will never leave your side."

"Not me. *Her.*" She grabbed his hands and placed them on her belly.

The baby responded with an offended kick.

Edmund swallowed, but did not remove his hands from her belly. His face was inches from hers, his mouth close enough to kiss, the warmth of his fingers sending a delicious shiver across her suddenly sensitive skin.

"Every morning," he said softly, his breath caressing her cheek. "You were my only thought." He tilted closer. "Every night, you were my only thought." His lips brushed her cheekbone. "Every moment of every day, you were my only thought."

She held her breath, unable to move. "And now?"

He leaned back, keeping both hands on her belly. "Now you both are."

"Well, if it isn't Mr. Blackpool," came a sharp, nettled voice as Sarah's mother emerged from the corridor. "Isn't this a surprise."

Edmund rose to his feet. "Mrs. Fairfax. It is lovely to see you again after so much time."

Sarah's mother wrinkled her nose. "I thought you were dead."

Edmund's smile was frigid, but he made no reply.

Sarah couldn't blame him. Her mother's implication had been anything but subtle. For her own selfish purposes, she would have preferred her daughter's fiancé to be dead rather than lose a marital connection to a dukedom—and the riches it inferred.

"How is *your* family, Edmund?" Sarah put in

quickly, hoping to deflect the awkwardness of her mother's obvious displeasure at the miracle of his return. "I have agonized over not being able to visit them. Your dear parents have suffered so terribly in your absence. That is one homecoming I would have loved to witness."

Edmund's gaze slowly tracked back to hers, his expression unreadable. "They don't know I'm back."

Her jaw dropped. "What? You haven't told them?"

"I came straight to you. You were the one I needed most."

She blushed as warmth flooded her. "Well, you must go to them immediately. Your mother has needed *you* the most. She commissioned a gravestone in your honor and spends nearly every waking moment kneeling before it."

Pain flashed through Edmund's eyes.

"You are right." He held out his hand, a crooked smile on his lips. "Come with me. We shall go together."

CHAPTER 5

*E*dmund gritted his teeth against clatter of his brother's horses and carriage. Sarah would not be joining them. She'd felt her presence would be a distraction—and she was undoubtedly correct—but he hated to leave her so soon after finding her again. Even a few days apart left an ache in his soul even his family could not completely fill.

The carriage crossed into Kent. Thank God. Sweat soaked into his clothes despite the chill wind. The noise of the road and the smell of the horses sucked him back into the battlefield no matter how hard he fought to stay in the present. Safe. With his brother. Yet he still could not relax.

He'd shared the full day's carriage ride with his twin. The one with which he had once shared everything—his days, his looks, his thoughts. His very identity.

But they were no longer identical.

Aside from the prosthetic limb replacing his right leg below the knee, Bartholomew still looked every bit as dapper as he always had. Before the war, Edmund had never once managed to look more stylish and sophisticated than his brother.

He still wasn't.

Despite Bartholomew's missing limb, he seemed very much together. He was happy, peaceful, amiable... even *married*. His wife was apparently involved in dozens of charity projects across the country, and Bartholomew was up to his elbows in work right along with her. Happily.

To say married life agreed with him was like saying water agreed with fishes. The loving glances they exchanged, the little touches, the jokes only the two of them understood.

A year ago, Edmund had been the one who could finish his brother's sentences. Now he didn't know his twin at all.

This trip was supposed to fix that. Bartholomew's wife Daphne had explained that of course Sarah must reject Edmund's invitation to accompany him—the elder Blackpools didn't even know she was pregnant. Sarah's condition had needed to remain secret if she wished to escape the worst of public ruination. His parents had no idea.

Perhaps he ought not to tell them. Not yet. One shock at a time, if you please.

As they rattled along the country roads, Edmund did his best not to stare at his brother. To go from inseparable to miles and months away... Being back in each other's company was strange, glorious, overwhelming.

Daphne had refused to join their party, despite being from the region herself. The long, snow-dusted carriageway between London and Maidstone would be the perfect opportunity for the brothers to reacquaint themselves.

But Edmund didn't feel reacquainted. He felt more lost than ever.

He had dreamed of being rescued. Of coming

home. Of returning to his carefree life of devil-may-care scrapes with his brother and stealing illicit kisses from Sarah. Of having his old life back. The life he'd longed for.

That life was gone.

If Bartholomew was living under vastly different circumstances, so was everyone else. Oliver had apparently inherited an earldom whilst fighting Boney's forces. He, too, was married now, as was Xavier Grey—who had apparently leg-shackled himself to a bluestocking, of all creatures. 'Twas dizzying. Every one of Edmund's determined-bachelor childhood friends had gotten married and moved on.

Everyone except Ravenwood.

Edmund supposed he ought to be grateful. If he really had succumbed to his wounds on the battlefield, the last thing he would've wanted was for Sarah, or the child he hadn't known existed, to suffer in his absence.

He knew without asking that Ravenwood would not have undertaken such an act lightly. The duke was the sole member of their roguish group who had always believed in love. Who had sworn he'd never wed without it. And yet he'd been willing to forgo that lifelong dream in order to rescue Sarah.

Unless...

Edmund straightened. Eight months was a long time. His friends and family had truly believed he was dead. Edmund swallowed. *Had* Ravenwood formed an attachment to Sarah? Might the duke be in love with Edmund's bride?

He shook the insidious thought from his head. The twisting in his stomach was exactly why he eschewed thinking about the past. It didn't matter. Neither did the future—that was an ephemeral dream that could be snatched away in the space of a breath.

All anyone could count on was the present. That was the one thing he had any control over at all.

"Where was your wedding?" he said aloud to escape the tumult in his head. He would focus on his brother. This was their opportunity to get back a little of what they'd lost.

Bartholomew seemed to glow at the memory. "We had the ceremony in All Saints Church, where Daphne's father had been vicar for so many years. I think it helped her feel like he was there with us."

Edmund nodded at the inadvertent reminder that he was not the only one who had suffered loss. Life had not been easy for him these past months. Perhaps it hadn't been easy for anybody.

He just wished he hadn't missed so much of it. Good or bad. If his brother was to go through a painful recovery, if his friends were to get leg-shackled at every turn, if Sarah was to find herself unexpectedly pregnant and frightened out of her mind, he wished he could have been there, sharing their joy and suffering right along with them.

Not hundreds of miles away with a hole in his chest and no way to get home.

He stole a sidelong glance at his brother's false limb. Trussed up as it was in expensive boots and tailored stockings, there was no hint that the prosthesis was not a real leg. Bartholomew himself showed no hint that he was less whole than he had been before. If anything, he seemed larger, more outgoing, more ebullient. Bartholomew was no cripple. He was cockier than ever.

Edmund couldn't have been prouder. "Your recovery was a miracle... and, I imagine, a surfeit of hard work. We're all fortunate someone found you on the battlefield and was able to get you to safety."

His brother swallowed and glanced away.

Edmund frowned. His brother fiddled with the reins quite convincingly, but Edmund had known his identical twin for their entire lives. Bartholomew was *hiding* something. From Edmund. His throat grew thick.

They had never held secrets from each other. Not once.

It felt even more like a betrayal than being left behind.

"How is Sarah?" Bartholomew asked suddenly, his voice falsely jovial.

A change in topics. Edmund forced his tight shoulders to relax. If his brother wished to avoid the subject, so be it. Lord knew, Edmund had no wish to discuss the war. Nor did he desire to spend his first days back arguing with the people he loved most.

"She's worried," he admitted. "We have no money and no place to live. Once we've wed, I intend to ask our parents if they wouldn't mind if we—"

"Oh, good Lord, no." Bartholomew nearly choked with horrified laughter. "No new marriage wants for our mother's unflagging eye. Stay in London. You *do* have a place to live."

"That's kind of you, brother, but your townhouse—"

"*Your* townhouse. You still have it."

"Unlikely," Edmund scoffed. "I left the bank instructions to settle accounts because I never meant to keep that place indefinitely. What money I had would have vanished quickly with the cost of the rent and servants. I'm all to pieces, brother. Not a penny to my name. I couldn't even sell back my commission to the army. The government has no idea I'm alive, much less home."

"*I* paid it," his twin said softly. "I not only sold my commission, I received additional funds due to the severity of my wounds while in service. Not just that. During the bedridden months of recovery, I made several risky and foolish investments—some of which paid off quite handsomely."

Edmund stared at him. "What are you saying?"

"The money you had in your accounts when I returned home from war is still there. All your *things* are still there. One of your servants is still there, keeping the place tidy. I thought you were dead, but I couldn't bring myself to dispose of your belongings. So I chose the cowardly path, and purchased the townhouse outright so I wouldn't have to erase your memory. It's all still yours, brother. To do with what you will. I'm only sorry I couldn't have done more. If I had so much as suspected you were still alive…"

His townhouse? His accounts? Edmund's heart was hammering far too quickly to allow for speech. On the one hand, he had never been one for accepting charity. On the other hand, this was his *twin*. Doing what brothers do: Looking out for one another. This changed everything.

His head swam. He had a place to live. Sarah and the baby had a place to live! His townhouse was small, but they would only be a family of three. With the right investments, they might one day live very comfortably indeed.

Might.

Then again, tomorrow he could contract consumption and never live to know his child's face. Such were the vagaries of Fate. He never knew what the wind would bring him or whisk away.

Edmund pushed the thought out of his mind. The future was unwritten. All he cared about was now, and right now he and his wife and child possessed a townhouse in which to live. That was all that mattered.

His spirits lifted further as Bartholomew drove his carriage into Maidstone and up the manicured path to their parents' country house. Nor did he miss the irony. As a young man, Edmund had found his father overbearing and his mother cloying. After the past eight months, he would happily submit to any amount of browbeating or cheek-pinching they chose to deliver.

His mother was already bustling out the door at the sight of her son's carriage stopping at the front gate. "Bartholomew! If you had but mentioned that you might visit, I would have prepared a feast for you and Daphne. I shall send the maids to market at once and insist—"

Edmund and his brother leaped down from the carriage at the same time. Just like they'd done for nearly six-and-twenty years, their boots hit the snow-specked path at the exact same moment.

His mother gasped. The blood drained from her face.

Edmund raced forward just as she swayed into a faint, and caught her in his arms.

His mother frequently fainted (often unconvincingly) when subjected to a sudden shock. He had always found her flair for the dramatic both irritating and embarrassing. This time, however, he was surprised to discover that he had missed it.

His swooning mother felt like home.

Edmund's wide-eyed father raced from the house looking thinner and much older since last Edmund saw him. Before Edmund could do more than grin delightedly at his father, his mother sprang out of his arms with the agility of a dancer and clapped her hands with glee.

"I *told* you he would come home!" she chortled in her husband's direction. She spun back to Edmund and pinched his cheeks as tears streamed down her own. "You are far too thin. You must eat! I'll have the cook make... I'll have him make *all* your favorite foods. Oh, Edmund, I *knew* you would come home. I knew it, I knew it!"

"When did you return, son?" his father asked, his glistening eyes betraying his restrained pleasure. "Could you not have written?"

"Of course he could not," his mother snapped. "If he could've written, he would've done so. He's *here*, which is a hundred times more important than having written." She beamed at Edmund. "Now that you're here, you shan't leave again. My heart couldn't possibly handle losing you a second time. You wouldn't make your mother go through that again, would you?"

Bartholomew raised his brows. "A townhouse in London is hardly the same as abandoning you, Mother. It takes less than a day to get from London to Maidstone if—"

"Oh, shush. Now that you're married, you don't have time for your mother. But Edmund! Edmund has all the time in the world. He'll live here—of course he'll live here. Bartholomew, you and Daphne could live here, too. There's room for all of us. I don't see any reason to live in London when you could live right here, in the chambers across from mine."

"We'll stay the night at least," Bartholomew said. "But we're here for a visit, not to live. I'm leaving it up to Edmund how much time he can spare."

"You're a bad son. A horrid son. But I forgive you everything because you brought me Edmund. Come inside, both of you. How are you going to eat if you're standing around the front porch like a flock of hens? The footmen will carry your things inside, don't you worry about that. Just march yourselves to the table and let me ring for some tea."

"Mother, has it ever occurred to you that grown, married men might not *wish* to live in their parents' house?" Bartholomew asked as he trailed her toward the dining room.

"What a foolish thing to think. Only you would say something so inane. Of course children wish to live close to their parents. Why wouldn't they? If for some reason you prefer privacy over your own parents, young man, there's no need to go gallivanting all over England to find it. There are no less than half a dozen perfectly suitable homes right here in Maidstone available for purchase or to let. A mile or two is more than far enough to live from one's family. Don't you think so, Edmund?"

He opened his mouth.

She waved his words away. "Of course you do. You're the sensible one. When Bartholomew goes on holiday with his 'crusading' wife, you'll stay right here with us where you belong. Hear me, Bartholomew? Your brother *wants* to stay home. Bachelor men aren't nearly as persnickety as you married men are."

Edmund cleared his throat. "As the fates would have it, Mother, I won't be a bachelor for much longer. Miss Sarah Fairfax and I are to be married."

"Are you?" His mother clasped her hands together and looked perilously close to swooning anew. "That's wonderful! You'll stay here for the length of your engagement—How long are you thinking? Two months? Three?—and that lovely girl can stop by every single week so that I can help her plan the festivities. A June wedding means hydrangea and peonies, I should say, and perhaps a snapdragon or two to help balance the color. Oh, what fun this shall be to plan!"

Edmund glanced at his brother, who simply held up his hands and took a less-than-subtle step back. Bartholomew was here as supporting troops, but Edmund would need to lead the charge.

"Actually..." He cleared his throat. He was just going to have to say it. "I'm afraid it won't be a long engagement. Sarah is... in a family way, and we must perform the ceremony as soon as possible. The babe will be born within a fortnight."

His father stared at him. "*When* did you say you got back?"

Edmund was saved from awkward explanations by his mother fainting directly into her husband's arms.

"Why didn't she tell us?" his mother wailed from her semi-prone position. "I have been a grandmother for *months* and hadn't the least idea. How will I ever forgive her?"

"There is nothing to forgive," Edmund snapped, belatedly realizing the depths of the predicament Sarah had found herself in. "You know as well as I that an unmarried woman cannot be seen to be with child if she ever wishes to present her face to Society again. Worse, she thought I was dead. By confessing her situation to you—or to anyone—she would have destroyed any opportunity to save the baby's fate."

His mother wiggled free from her husband's arms. "But when would you have—"

"Bruges," he answered. "Just before Waterloo. She joined me for my last day of leave."

His father arched a brow.

Edmund colored. "During her stay, I asked her to marry me and she acquiesced. I regret that my actions caused her to suffer. My feelings have not changed, but the war disrupted our timeline."

Disrupted it so badly that Sarah was forced to the altar within scant weeks of her expected delivery. She could not have waited any longer, he realized. She was out of choices and out of time.

"In that case, of course the two of you will live here," his mother said briskly, her eyes softening. "Trying to avoid scandal in London is like trying to avoid heat in the summertime. Bring her here at once. She'll feel right at home. We'll be two peas in a pod, planning a wedding and a christening. Why, I'm happy to set up a nursery in any room that she wants. The chamber between hers and mine will do nicely. I've got nothing else to do. I'll be the most helpful, loving, and attentive grandmother you lovebirds could ever dream of!"

Edmund stared at his well-meaning mother in growing dismay. It was good to be home, but allowing his mother to smother his bride with unceasing attentions was the last thing they needed. The *first* thing they needed was the privacy—and the time—to get to know each other again.

Correction: the first step in the battle was to get married.

CHAPTER 6

Within hours of having returned from his visit to his parents, Edmund had given enough orders and commissioned enough supplies to feel like the general of an army.

His townhouse (long live Bartholomew!) would be the base for Operation Wife and Baby. There wasn't quite enough money to employ more than a skeletal crew of servants, but how much trouble could a tiny infant be?

Once a few investments paid off, they could hire governesses or nannies or wet nurses or whatever the baby needed. Until then, Edmund and Sarah would simply have to be battalion leaders. A team. A solid, united front against the world.

Or at least against soiled nappies.

Bearing a folded parchment on a silver tray, Edmund's manservant entered what had once been Edmund's study and was now a makeshift nursery. A cradle would arrive within the week, as would a beggaring amount of linens and white cotton baby gowns and suitable toys. And a pair of rocking chairs had been commissioned to match the cradle.

The housekeeper had suggested most of the items,

for which Edmund was deeply grateful. He knew nothing about being a husband and even less about being a father to a small child. His own past gave no insight. He and his brother had been nearly eight years old before they could finally slip out from under their mother's watchful eye to engage in manly pursuits with their father. Hunting. Fishing. Boxing.

Those things would come later. The first year would be the hardest. Or perhaps the most dull. When did babies begin talking and playing? When they were two years of age? Three? Perhaps that was why he and his twin hadn't engaged their father's interest until they were much older. They had been boring.

No matter. Even if his child was nothing more than a pretty little doll at first, he would not abandon Sarah to do the rearing herself. Nor should she have to. His fists clenched. If he had more money, she wouldn't have had to lift a finger—most gentlewomen had little reason to interact with their offspring.

But Sarah was not most gentlewomen and Edmund was not a gentleman at all. If he were, he wouldn't have taken her innocence and left her with child. Nor would he have stolen her out from the arms of a duke, or forced her to live in renovated bachelor apartments while he made rash investments in hopes of a large windfall.

He didn't wish Sarah to have a comfortable existence. He wished her to have a marvelous one. He wanted to surround her with riches and luxury and pleasure. She had given up her chance at being a duchess… for him. The least he could do was treat her like one.

Edmund had just finished dragging the boxes of old ledgers from his study into the cubby beneath the stairwell when he recalled both the presence of his footman—who would have been more than happy to do the heavy lifting himself—and the missive upon his platter.

Cheeks burning, Edmund snatched the letter up from the tray and tried to feign as though it were not strange at all for him to have automatically thrown himself into servants' work.

Edmund sighed. He would be gossip fodder by nightfall.

When he'd left for war, he doubted he'd ever wondered where items were stored when they were not in use, much less have been aware of the existence of storage areas beneath staircases. Or the best way to lift a heavy crate so that one's back did not spasm with agony upon the morrow.

He would not think of the past, Edmund reminded himself as he inspected the letter. He would think only of Sarah. And... Ravenwood? Edmund broke the familiar seal and began to read.

BLACKPOOL,

Come to Ravenwood House at once. Urgent matter requires your immediate presence.

Dress nicely.

Ravenwood

EDMUND REREAD the contents a second time before he was certain he'd understood it correctly. When had the letter been delivered? He glanced at the clock upon the mantel. Perhaps a half hour past? If he hadn't been so busy doing footmen's work, Edmund could already *be* at Ravenwood House.

Jaw clenched, he strode into his bedchamber to

make himself as presentable as possible. Surprisingly, his coxcomb brother had not thought a valet to be an essential part of Edmund's staff. He had a footman, a cook, and a housekeeper, but no one to tell him whether the waistcoats he'd purchased four years ago were still at the height of fashion—or likely to make him a laughingstock.

There was no time to worry about such things, nor did they warrant his attention. He had decided toward the beginning of the war that anything that wouldn't matter in a month's time didn't deserve to matter at all. That pragmatism had gotten him through the worst of it.

An unfashionable waistcoat was the least of his concerns.

He cleaned and dressed as quickly as he could before descending to the street to flag a hack. Bartholomew had in fact continued paying for the upkeep of Edmund's old horses, but this morning Edmund had sold everything and split the profit with his brother.

Someday, he and Sarah would have the finest steeds and finest carriages in all of London. For the next few months, however, they were unlikely to leave the nursery. That savings was better spent in investments that could double or triple in value over time.

He hoped.

The moment the hack dropped him off at Ravenwood House, the butler was already opening the door to grant him entrance.

Edmund frowned, but did not slow his pace. He assumed the staff would be less than pleased with his interruption of the duke's plans to take a wife, but they were doing a masterful job at keeping their expressions clear of rancor or judgment.

A footman led Edmund not toward Ravenwood's study, but toward the billiard room. Rather, toward the back parlor where the duke had tried to wed Edmund's bride.

His heart quickened as he entered the room. The same people were present. Sarah and Ravenwood, at the altar. The vicar. Edmund's own brother—this time accompanied by his wife Daphne and... Sarah's elder brother Anthony?

"What is this?" Edmund demanded, his voice hoarse with fear and fury.

Ravenwood stepped forward. "You're getting married. I apologize, but there wasn't enough time to summon your parents up from Kent for the ceremony. The vicar must leave for Derby within the hour, and I know you wish to take care of this matter promptly."

Edmund blinked, then swung his baffled gaze to Sarah.

"He used his influence to have your request for a special license granted," she murmured low enough so only he could hear. "Considering this vicar witnessed what happened last time... He thought it best to involve the least number of persons as possible."

Ravenwood thought it best. Edmund's teeth clenched behind his frigid smile. He forced his tight muscles to relax.

Would it matter a month from now who had helped procure the special license, and how? No, it would not. All that mattered was Sarah. Miraculously, she would be his, at last.

"You may take your seat," he couldn't resist ordering Ravenwood, before turning to the vicar. "Please begin as soon as you're ready."

The vicar nodded.

Edmund took Sarah's hands and didn't let go.

She was beautiful. Her eyes were tired and her limbs had swollen and her stomach was large enough to birth a baby elephant... *His* baby elephant. There was nowhere else he'd rather be than by her side, holding her hands in his.

It didn't matter whether either one of them was ready to marry or to start a family. That was what they'd been given. What they had wanted. If not like this.

The vicar turned to Edmund. "Have you a ring for your bride?"

Sarah's fingers flinched and grew cold in Edmund's hands. The room fell silent.

Ravenwood leapt up from his seat. "You are welcome to use the—"

"I have a ring," Edmund said quietly.

He released Sarah's hands just long enough to reach into his waistcoat pocket and pull out the ring he had purchased in Bruges after Sarah had boarded her passenger ship back to England.

The reason it hadn't been stolen when he'd been left for dead on the battlefield was because he hadn't been willing to leave it in his camp—or even in his pockets. He had tied it about the arm closest to his heart with the ribbon Sarah had used to fasten her stockings. For him, it had represented a piece of the past and his dreams for the future.

Back when he'd believed in such things.

He slid the ring on Sarah's finger with steady hands that belied the trepidation gripping his heart. His desire to wed her had never once flagged. It had only grown stronger day by day, month by month.

Did she feel the same? Or for her, did this feel more like an ending than a new beginning?

It was too late for doubt. The vicar was nearly done.

"Forasmuch as Mr. Edmund Blackpool and Miss Sarah Fairfax have consented together in holy wedlock, and have witnessed the same before God and this company, and have declared the same by giving and receiving a ring, and by joining hands…" The vicar's voice rang out clear and true. "I pronounce that they are man and wife."

Man and wife. Edmund's heart swelled. He wanted nothing more than to pull her into his arms, to kiss her senseless and thoroughly. But he'd already done quite enough to tarnish her reputation. Kisses could wait until they were alone tonight.

Hands clapped against his back as their friends surrounded them to give their well-wishes. Edmund's ears roared from the noise and the feel of so many hands upon him at once. Everyone, it seemed, wished to hug him.

Ravenwood apologized again for being unable to fetch Edmund's parents in time. And for offering up his own ring when Edmund needed no such intervention.

Edmund shook his head. He didn't care what Ravenwood did with his ring. Edmund was finally married to Sarah.

"Where is Xavier?" he asked. "Could he not attend, or were we too intimate of a party?"

Daphne shook her head. "He's in Chelmsford, I'm afraid."

"Entertaining a bluestocking," Bartholomew put in with a salacious wink.

Edmund couldn't help but laugh at the image. "And Oliver? Now that he's Earl of Carlisle, he must be in London. His presence is required in the House of Lords."

"He… didn't wish to intrude," Ravenwood said, a touch too diplomatically.

"Intrude?" Edmund's brow furrowed. "He's been one of my best friends for as long as I've known him. One of *our* best friends. When has he ever chosen not to accompany us in anything?"

Daphne sent a pointed glance at the duke, who in turn sent a desperate glance toward Bartholomew, who lowered his eyes and looked away.

"Ah." Edmund's flesh ran cold. "The secret."

Bartholomew glanced over at him, startled. "You know?"

"There obviously *is* one. Since everyone seems privy but me, you might as well come out with it. Why would my childhood friend have refused to attend my wedding?"

"He didn't refuse," Ravenwood said with a sigh. "He did it for you. He didn't want you to look back on your wedding day and feel the experience had been soured because of his presence."

"Soured how? He's one of my best—"

"Waterloo," Bartholomew interrupted, his chin up and his tone flat. "You had just been shot in the chest. The wound appeared mortal. But I refused to leave you there to die. So I raced as fast as I could to where I'd seen you fall…"

"—and ran directly in the path of the cannon fire," Daphne finished, linking her arm with her husband's. She lay her cheek to his shoulder.

Ravenwood nodded. "By the time Carlisle got there, you both had lost too much blood and the French were closing in. There was no time to save you both. Not with all the bullets and cannons firing in the air. Carlisle risked his foolish hide by even trying."

The pieces clicked into place. Dully, Edmund nodded his understanding. "Oliver had to choose."

Bartholomew grabbed his arm. "He wanted to save us both, but—"

"He chose you." Edmund closed his eyes as months of pain and fear and hunger and desperation washed over him. He had felt furious. Frightened. Abandoned. And as it turned out, he truly had been. "I see."

"Edmund—"

"I'm not angry with you, brother," he said tiredly. His twin had tried to save him. That was how he'd gotten his leg blown off in the first place. It was more than Edmund could handle right now. "If you'll excuse me, the only thing I really want right now is some time alone with my new bride."

He couldn't imagine what she must think. Sarah had been quiet during the entire conversation. He glanced over his shoulder and frowned. She was not behind him. He pushed his friends and brother aside to cast his frantic gaze about the entire empty room.

Sarah was gone.

CHAPTER 7

An hour later, Sarah accepted a steaming cup of tea from a little silver tray and settled back against a mountain of soft pillows in Miss Katherine Ross's townhouse. "Thank you so much for taking me in. I didn't know where else to turn. None of my friends know that I'm increasing, so I couldn't go knocking upon their doors in this condition."

And she'd needed to go *somewhere*. She needed a chance to collect herself. To think. To plan. And it was impossible to think whilst surrounded by her family, her friends. Edmund's unexpected reappearance had thrown them all into a tizzy.

Like her, they were overjoyed at his return. Unlike her, they didn't have to worry about what to do next. How to rekindle romance whilst eight and a half months pregnant. How to live happily ever after when hunger pangs kept them from sleeping. How to give her child the many opportunities of London on extremely limited purse strings.

"Having you spend the night is my pleasure." Miss Ross poured a dram of milk into her tea and smiled at Sarah. "Anthony might be a rapscallion and a shameless rogue, but he is also a dear friend. The least I can do is open my home to his sister."

Sarah's eyes narrowed at her teacup, but she made no further comment.

Her brother Anthony was indeed a rapscallion and a shameless rogue. Miss Ross, on the other hand, was a young, eccentric patroness of the arts—and first cousin to the Duke of Lambley. Sarah could scarcely imagine how her brother and the elegant Miss Ross had ever crossed paths, much less become fast friends.

"Anthony?" Miss Ross's great aunt asked as her trembling hands brought her teacup closer to her lips. "You don't mean that charming Mr. Fairfax, do you, Kate?"

"Yes, dear heart. The very one." Miss Ross smiled indulgently at her great aunt, despite having answered this same query three times since Sarah's arrival on her doorstep.

If Sarah found it hard to imagine Anthony moving in the same circles as Miss Ross, 'twas even more difficult to imagine him having cause to make the acquaintance of Miss Ross's Great Aunt Havens.

Then again, Anthony worked in mysterious ways. He knew lots of women. Had gambled with most of their husbands. Once, when he'd thought Sarah wasn't listening, he'd alluded to very nearly winning a young lady as a prize in a game of chance.

Sarah couldn't imagine Miss Ross in so ignominious a position, but one never knew with Anthony. Perhaps he'd won Great Aunt Havens during a midnight game of hazard.

As the hot tea eased her parched throat, Sarah allowed herself to relax a little.

What she'd wanted—what she'd *needed*—was time to think. Now that she was safely wed, she could finally spare a moment to do so. Her child would be born legitimate... and to his rightful father. Sarah had missed him so much.

She desperately wanted them to have a happy marriage. She'd already destroyed his trust by standing at the altar with another man. Even without that, she'd ruined his dreams for an idyllic reunion by carrying a child in her belly—she'd seen the look in his eyes when he saw her. Shock. Horror. Disillusionment. He hadn't returned to a lover. He'd had disappointment and fatherhood thrust upon him.

Sarah had a scant fortnight to take stock of her new situation and plan for the future before the baby was born. But she had only tonight to collect her thoughts and come up with a plan. She and Edmund had already been apart for far too long. Her greatest fear was losing him again. Not to distance, this time, but to unhappiness. Their new life would not be the romantic romp it once was. She swallowed hard.

Now that they were back together, he might no longer want her.

"I would ask if it's a man," Miss Ross said with a smile, "but it's always a man. The ring on your finger makes me suspect marital bliss has proved elusive?"

"My husband has proved elusive." Despite her fears, a delicious chill slid down Sarah's spine at the words *my husband*. "He was a soldier, and had gone missing after Waterloo. We all thought he was dead until he showed up less than a week ago, just in time to stop my marriage to someone else."

Miss Ross's eyes widened. "Who on earth were you going to marry?"

Sarah twisted her ring. "The Duke of Ravenwood."

Miss Ross very nearly spit tea into her lap.

"Ravenwood?" Mrs. Havens repeated in her

querulous voice. "You don't mean Lawrence Pembroke, the duke's son, do you?"

"He's duke now, Aunt." Miss Ross patted her lips with a handkerchief then burst out laughing. "*Ravenwood*. Jilted!"

Sarah tilted her head. "I take it you know him?"

"Know him? I would've given a monkey to watch it happen."

"*Kate*," Mrs. Havens chastised her niece. "How many times have I told you not to say—"

"Fine. I would've paid 'five hundred pounds' to see the look on his face."

Sarah shifted uncomfortably, regretting she'd ever confided her story. Ravenwood was one of the best men she had ever known. "You dislike the duke?"

"Dislike him?" Miss Ross chortled. "Good God, no. Ravenwood is a beautiful, solemn, lofty, mysterious, utterly *unflappable* automaton of ducal restraint. I've never seen him smile or even frown. He just nods gravely and deals dispassionately with whatever comes his way. An automaton, I tell you. His lack of passion is utterly disturbing."

"She's quite taken by him," Mrs. Havens whispered conspiratorially. "In case it's not obvious."

Miss Ross snorted. "He fascinates me, is all. The mystery of it. I've never known someone not to have *feelings*."

"He has feelings," Sarah protested.

"Does he?" Miss Ross arched a brow. "Did he fall deeply in love with you, then? Is that why you were at the altar?"

"No, but—"

"Was he crushed when your former lover returned? Did his piercing emerald eyes glisten with manly tears as he begged you not to leave him, lest his heart be forever broken?"

"No, but—"

"Can you say, with any degree of honesty, that he particularly cared one way or the other which groom you took to be your husband that day?"

Sarah tightened her fists and glared at her hostess in mute defiance.

Miss Ross leaned back in satisfaction. "There you have it. A classic automaton. All brain and no emotion. You should see him in the House of Lords."

Sarah's shoulders twitched. "You've watched him in the House of Lords?"

Miss Ross grinned. "I've watched everyone in the House of Lords since I was old enough to sneak in."

"Kate hasn't always behaved outrageously," Mrs. Havens assured Sarah, sotto voce. "The few months before she learned to crawl were quite idyllic indeed."

"Bah, Aunt!" Miss Ross snapped a playful handkerchief toward her great aunt's knee. "I'm sure I found ways to be outrageous even then."

Sarah found herself smiling despite her best effort not to. Miss Ross hadn't meant to be disrespectful to Ravenwood. She didn't know him. She simply said precisely what she was thinking, the moment it occurred to her.

She shook her head. "I suppose you're the opposite of an automaton?"

Miss Ross affected a haughty expression. "I should hope so. I'm deeply emotional about absolutely everything. I even have deeply emotional feelings about the roasted chestnuts in this bowl and the currant biscuits on that plate. I will challenge you to a duel if you dare consume more than your portion."

"I'm...*pregnant*," Sarah protested, daring to use the more vulgar term.

"That's why you get half and not a third, as would

be more fair." Miss Ross tossed a saucy grin at her aunt. "See? I share. Occasionally."

Sarah widened her eyes and pointed over Miss Ross's shoulder. "Is that *another* tray of chestnuts?"

Miss Ross gasped in delight and twisted in her chair to see.

Sarah lifted the plate of currant biscuits off of the tray and placed it atop her belly for quick access. When Miss Ross spun back around with narrowed eyes, Sarah's mouth was delightfully full of biscuit.

"Well done, Miss Fairfax," Miss Ross said approvingly.

"Blackpool," Sarah mumbled around a mouthful of delicious biscuit. "I'm married now."

"You poor thing," Miss Ross agreed with a shiver. "God willing, I shall never fall into the parson's trap. I'd make a terrible wife. You, however… Tell me how you ended up leg-shackled, and what I can do to avoid it."

"I fell in love," she admitted miserably. "From the first day I met him. He was brash and audacious and confident and handsome and everything a girl like me thought she wanted in a man."

Miss Ross nodded pensively. "It turned out he wasn't what you'd thought?"

"It turned out he was exactly what I'd thought. The daredevil side of him I'd found so magnetic was the same impetus that sent him off to war and very nearly got him killed." Sarah bit her lip, then met Miss Ross's gaze. "I've already lost him once. I can't go through that again. I *won't*."

Miss Ross arched her brows. "And yet you married him."

"I love him," Sarah said simply. "I always have. The man I gave my heart to was warm and tender and loving. But the man who came home, I cannot recognize. He's colder now. He didn't ask for my hand. He informed me—and the Duke of Ravenwood—that I was his, and that was final. There was no mention of love. He has never actually stated that the feeling was mutual."

Miss Ross frowned. "Yet *you* married him for love?"

"Do you think me foolish? My parents certainly do. But even if I take my heart out of consideration, Edmund is still my child's father. Would you be able to keep your child from his father?"

Miss Ross recoiled as if Sarah had flung spiders at her. "Bite your tongue. I wouldn't have a child at all."

"Kate has a horror of childbirthing," Mrs. Havens whispered to Sarah. "Anthony Fairfax had to promise her you were still a fortnight from any danger before Kate was half willing to invite you to tea, much less stay the night."

"Aunt, *honestly*," Miss Ross huffed. "We're discussing Mrs. Blackpool's private matters, not mine."

Sarah blinked in startled confusion before she recalled that "Mrs. Blackpool" meant *her,* and not Edmund's mother. She hid a smile behind her napkin. "Call me Sarah. Please."

"Brilliant." Miss Ross beamed at her and held out her hand. "You may call me Katherine."

Amused at the odd gesture, Sarah lifted her fingers to shake Katherine's hand—and gasped in mock outrage when Katherine took the opportunity to snatch what was left of the biscuit plate from atop Sarah's belly instead.

"Eat some chestnuts," Katherine advised her around a mouthful of biscuit. "Less fattening."

Sarah's answering laugh was hollow. "That is another problem. I have always known that Edmund chose me because I was pretty to look at. You might notice I'm no longer a diamond of the first water."

Frowning, Katherine set down the plate of biscuits. "Pregnant women are *supposed* to be fat. In case nobody's told you, there's a baby in there."

Sarah rubbed her face. "Precisely the problem. Edmund never asked to be saddled with *this*."

He had wanted someone who could adorn his arm. Someone to gaze up at him with stars in her eyes and welcome him to her bed.

She had worshipped him. She still did. He was strong and dashing and unpredictable. Their every encounter took her breath away.

No, they had never exchanged *I love you*s. Their encounters had been too exciting, too passionate, to waste them with words.

When she had arrived in Bruges eight months ago, neither one of them had cared whether theirs was a love match. Their physical attraction was impossible to deny. His eyes had devoured her with such intensity, 'twas a wonder they hadn't made love right there on the dock.

She spread her fingers over her swollen belly. The white marks stretching up her stomach would never go away. Her hips would widen, her feet had flattened, her ankles were alarmingly thick.

Now that the carnal hunger was gone, what did they have left? Would they be strong enough to survive everything the future now held?

CHAPTER 8

The endless squadrons of soot-stained row houses closed in on Edmund like the bloodthirsty troops of an invading army. London's noisy cobblestone streets, fetid waste pits, and imposing shields of solid brick surrounded him. Mocking him with their superior numbers. Gleefully concealing all traces of his bride.

Sarah was not at home. She was not at Edmund's home, she was not at Ravenwood House, she was not with her family. She wasn't *anywhere*.

"We going somewhere?" The hack driver spat into the street. "Or you paying me to rest my arse?"

Edmund slammed his fist against the moldy squab. "We're going somewhere."

The question was where.

He'd flagged down the hack not just because he had no carriage of his own, but because the streets had filled with so many pedestrians—beggars, pie makers, women with parasols, chimney boys—all bustling and banging into him and shouting to be heard over the clop of horses and the click of iron wheels against cobblestone that Edmund couldn't even *think*.

The drafty, open hack did little to block the overwhelming noise but at least Edmund wasn't constantly buffeted by so many hurrying people, hundreds of strange bodies elbowing and shoving.

The last time such a tide had rushed in and over him from all sides, he'd ended up facedown with a bullet in his chest. All he could hear were the racing footsteps, the urgent horse hooves, the shouts as storming soldiers slashed and shot and fell.

He fought the urge to cover his ears with his hands. He would *not* think of the past. He was in London, not Waterloo. He was in a hackney cab, not lying upon a blood-stained cart. The noise was the same, the chaos was the same, but he had to focus on the mission at all costs.

Find Sarah.

"Carlisle House," he said suddenly. "Take me to the Earl of Carlisle's estate."

The driver spat again and shook the reins.

Edmund leaned back against the carriage to avoid looking out at the street. Instead, he closed his eyes and summoned an image of Sarah. There was no doubt she had run.

His heart clenched. He hadn't meant to *frighten* her. That was the last thing he wished. He just wanted... he just wanted their old lives back. He wanted to be carefree and happy. He wanted *her* to gaze up at him like she used to, with her hazel eyes sparkling with love and her fingers entwined with his. He wanted the promises they'd made each other not to be dreams, but reality.

Reality, unfortunately, had other plans.

Sarah had run. There were few places she could run *to*. She was married now, and therefore the baby's legitimacy had been ensured, but that didn't mean Sarah could pay house calls on Polite Society the day after her wedding. Married or not, she was eight months pregnant and even the dullest of debutantes could perform simple math.

Thus, Oliver.

Oliver had chosen to leave Edmund bleeding to death on a foreign battlefield. Oliver had chosen to stay home, rather than to attend Edmund's wedding. If he thought Sarah needed rescuing, Oliver would have chosen to harbor Edmund's wife without a second thought.

Edmund rubbed the bridge of nose and sighed. *Did* Sarah need rescuing?

Before leaving for France, Edmund had never had to worry or care about anyone else's expectations. War was different, of course, in that there were different rules and fierce enemies and a new hierarchy. But none of that had been any problem. He was a crack shot with a rifle, became a brigadier in the blink of an eye—and he was the only soldier of his acquaintance whose love interest back home actually sailed to Bruges to spend the night in his arms.

Everything had been easy. His life had always been perfect.

Until a bullet shattered his rib and there were so many running, trampling footsteps, none of which cared a fig about the dying soldiers unable to rise from the blood-soaked ground...

"This is Carlisle House," said the driver. "That'll be an extra shilling for the delay."

Edmund tossed him a coin and leapt from the hack. His boots landed against the frozen grass with a soft crunch.

His tense muscles relaxed slightly. The row houses were too far away to see. The people were gone. The only sounds were the call of a misplaced winter robin and the fading clomp of the hack driver's departing carriage. Bless Oliver for owning enough land to have a bit of peace and quiet.

Edmund would still plant him a facer, though, if the earl was hiding Edmund's wife.

He strode up the walkway and rapped the heavy knocker against the front door. He couldn't remember the last time he'd been to Carlisle House. Oliver's father had always been earl, as well as a pompous drunkard. He and his son got on like Wellington and Bonaparte, so Oliver had spent the vast majority of his time at Ravenwood House or with one or both of the Blackpool brothers.

Lord knew a single afternoon of Edmund's mother hovering and cooing and forcing favorite meals down everyone's throats would make anyone feel as though he'd been mothered for decades.

The door swung open, revealing an elderly butler that Edmund wasn't quite certain if he recognized. He belatedly recalled he had no calling cards with which to present himself. Not that it mattered. If Sarah was inside, Edmund would happily take the earl's estate by force.

But first, he would try polite manners. "Edmund Blackpool to see the earl."

"Wait here, please."

Edmund laced his fingers behind his back to keep from clenching and unclenching them in anxiety and trepidation. If Oliver had Edmund's wife... he'd kill him. But if the earl did not? Where was there left to look?

The butler returned. "Come with me, sir. He's having dinner with his family, but has arranged another place setting for you."

Edmund frowned, but followed.

None of this made sense. If Oliver was harboring Edmund's wife, it seemed unlikely the earl would extend an invitation to the supper table. And it was odd that the butler had said Oliver was dining with his family, rather than with his new wife.

Oliver *had* no family. Edmund had no idea who the earl's wife was, but they couldn't have been married long enough to have a family. Edmund had started a trifle too soon, and even his bride still carried their child within her.

"Here you are, sir."

Edmund blinked at the four place settings and the modest offering upon the table. Oliver was already rising to his feet from the head of the table, as were the two beautiful, dark-haired women who had sat on either side.

"If you are not too dangerous to approach," Oliver said quietly, "I would very much like to apologize."

Edmund neither replied nor turned away.

"It is good to see you, Edmund. No—it is *wonderful* to see you. An answer to a prayer. You cannot know how much guilt, how many nightmares…"

Edmund met his eyes. "Bartholomew told me."

"Of course he did. He is your brother and you deserved to know. I would not have disrespected you further by keeping a secret."

Edmund's jaw worked. That did sound like Oliver, damn him. Honorable to a bloody fault.

Sarah would not be here.

"You didn't come to the wedding," he said instead.

"Your wedding was about *you*, not me or us." Oliver reached forward and grasped Edmund's hand. "It's so good to have you back. To see you *alive*. I had thought… We had all feared…"

Edmund did not pull his hand from Oliver's grasp. "Most of the fallen did not live to rise again."

Oliver's eyes glistened. "Oh, Edmund, I am *so* sorry. So wretchedly, inexcusably sorry—"

Edmund wrapped his arms about the earl. "If you had let my brother die, I would have killed you."

Oliver gave a choking laugh and hugged Edmund back. "I'm so glad you're home. Please say you'll stay for supper. Now that you're back, I'm not quite ready to let you out of my sight."

Edmund stepped back and nodded. He might as well stay for a meal. He hadn't eaten all day, and he had no idea where to go next. And despite his conflicted feelings about being left on the battlefield to die… it was good to see Oliver, too. Had Edmund been forced to choose between saving his brother and saving the earl, there would be no earldom.

Sometimes, there were no *right* choices. Just… choices.

Oliver puffed out his chest and gestured at the two ladies on either side. "It is my deep honor to present you to my wife Grace, and her mother, Mrs. Halton."

Edmund tried to hide his surprise. The women looked more like sisters than mother and daughter. Mrs. Halton was clearly the elder of the two, but old enough to have birthed a countess? He stepped forward to bow, and kiss both sets of fingers. "It is my pleasure."

Lady Carlisle's eyes shone. "No, the pleasure is mine. I'm so glad to actually meet you!"

Edmund jerked his startled gaze toward Oliver, who laughed as though he'd been waiting for this joke the entire time.

"Yes, I'm afraid she's American." Oliver slid a possessive arm about his wife's waist and kissed her temple. "But I love her anyway."

Lady Carlisle slapped him in the chest, but blushed becomingly.

Her mother flashed Edmund a rueful smile. "For

better or worse, I'm from right here in London. Although you can perhaps tell by my accent that my heritage is not as lofty as you're used to."

Edmund was suddenly grateful for the table. He was going to need to sit down after all. Oliver's story must be as astonishing as Edmund's own.

He waited until the ladies had retaken their seats before claiming his own. "What have I missed? Tell me everything."

A footman hurried forward to fill Edmund's plate with food.

"My father passed," Oliver began, "leaving me the title and more bills than the estate was worth."

"He needed an heiress," Lady Carlisle explained with a smile.

"Ah." Edmund nodded.

Lady Carlisle's smile widened. "I was not one."

Edmund's fork paused.

Mrs. Halton tilted her head toward her daughter. "I was in Pennsylvania at the time."

"Dying of consumption," Lady Carlisle clarified. "She needed emergency care if she was to survive, but we had no money."

"But my parents did." Mrs. Halton's cheeks flushed. "So I sent Grace to London in the hopes they'd offer her a dowry."

Lady Carlisle kissed her husband's cheek. "Before we were even married, Oliver sent a pirate to fetch my mother."

Edmund's fork clattered onto his plate. "Sent a what?"

"Blackheart," Mrs. Halton said dreamily.

Lady Carlisle's head spun around. "*Mama.*"

"Er, he was dreadful. Horrid." Mrs. Halton waved a slender hand in disdain. "Too much muscle and swagger for my tastes. A brute, really. So arrogant and strong…"

Lady Carlisle dropped her face into her hands, then glared at her husband. "This is your fault, you know. If Mama runs off with a pirate…"

"I would never run anywhere," Mrs. Halton protested.

"You ran to *America* when you were seventeen years old!"

"Well, it would have to be quite a pirate to tempt me away from all this. I have a family again." Mrs. Halton touched her daughter's cheek. "I have *you* again, Grace. I have no urge to go anywhere."

Oliver leaned forward to pin his gaze on Edmund. "What about you? It's good to see you, but… shouldn't you be with Sarah? I can't imagine you would leave her side if she were feeling unwell."

Edmund's chest tightened. "I would never leave her. Sarah left me."

CHAPTER 9

Tears sprang to Sarah's eyes as her nightrail-covered knee rammed into yet another block of antique furniture. *Blast*.

The problem wasn't disorientation from having slept in someone else's townhouse for a few nights. A low fire crackled behind the grate and bathed Sarah's bedchamber with a soft, warm glow.

The problem was Sarah's complete inability to walk in a straight line.

Somewhere around month six or seven, her ability to stroll had devolved into an unbecoming waddle. By month eight, she frequently found herself veering off into unexpected angles. Over the past week—*ouch!* Deuce it, why was there so much bloody furniture?—she had become so huge and ungainly that every time she took a step, she crashed into something.

The snow falling outside was beautiful and relaxing, or at least it would be if Sarah were capable of sleep. The baby kicked her at all hours of the day and night, and at least half of those well-placed kicks resulted in the immediate need to use a chamber pot. She had even begun dreaming about stomach pain, but the last several times she'd woken, her bladder had been empty.

Sarah washed her hands in the expensive porcelain basin on her bedside table without managing to upend either item, and decided to slip down to the kitchen in search of a bite to eat. Heaven help her, she was always hungry.

'Twas perhaps three or four in the morning. She didn't feel comfortable waking any servants just because she wanted something sweet, but dash it, she could not seem to go a single hour without yet another food craving.

The trick would be not tumbling down the staircase mid-route.

She shrugged a robe over her nightrail and lit a candle in the fireplace to light her way before she slowly eased open her chamber door.

When her foot landed on a squeaky floorboard, she covered her mouth to hide a giggle. The situation reminded her too much of sneaking into kitchens with Anthony in search of biscuits, when they were young children.

Sarah had just reached the staircase when a sudden cramp gripped her belly—and was just as quickly gone. She frowned and ran her hands over her stomach. It had almost felt like her womanly cramps, except of course she hadn't had one of those in eight months.

She counted slowly to one hundred, but the feeling didn't return. Instead, her stomach growled its impatience. The baby delivered a double kick, just to make certain Sarah was paying attention.

"Yes, fine, biscuits," she muttered at her belly and turned back toward the stairs.

This time, the sudden cramp was severe enough

to make her cry out and stumble against the banister to catch her breath.

Katherine's door flung open and she ran out into the corridor, wild-eyed. "What is it? What's happening?"

"I'm fine," Sarah gasped, clutching the banister for dear life. "I'm just…"

A stream of warm liquid splashed down her bare legs and onto Katherine's expensive wood floor.

Sarah's cheeks flamed with embarrassment. If only the banister would swallow her whole. She had *tried* to use the chamber pot. She would never live down the mortification of—

"*Ohh*," she moaned as another cramp seized her from the inside.

Another door flew open. Katherine's Great-Aunt Havens rushed into the corridor—and stepped right into the fresh warm puddle.

Sarah closed her eyes. This was beyond humiliation. This was—

"The baby," Mrs. Havens breathed. "It's coming *now*."

"Nooo," Katherine moaned and sagged against the wainscoting. "You *promised* you wouldn't do this until you'd gone back home. You gave me your solemn word."

"I'm sorry," Sarah gasped, clutching her belly. "I should have another fortnight…"

"You should get back into bed," Mrs. Havens said briskly, braving the wet puddle to wrap a bracing arm about Sarah's back. "Come. Let's get you settled. Kate, have the staff fetch hot water and clean cloths. You'll need them to—"

"Me?" Katherine blanched in horror. "I shall not be anywhere near a childbirthing. I'll be down at the closest pub, spending every coin I have on gin."

"Very well, then. Just wait in the corridor and summon the items I demand, as I ask for them. I will handle everything."

"You? But you haven't been a midwife in twenty years, Aunt. You can't possibly—"

"Kate. Who do you suppose will deliver this baby? Father Christmas? There isn't time to do anything else."

"Hot water," Katherine repeated as she raced toward the stairs. "Clean cloths. Back in a moment."

Sarah lay back in the bed and tried not to succumb to complete and utter panic.

Midwife. She didn't have a midwife. She didn't have *anything*. The baby clothes she had embroidered were at home at her parents'. Her tiny nest egg was at the Bank of England and could not be withdrawn without her presence. Her husband didn't even know she was *here*. She moaned. This was a disaster.

Katherine skidded back into the room with an armful of pristine white towels. Two footmen followed close behind, each carrying pails of steaming water. Katherine immediately sent them off for more.

"Here are the cloths, Aunt." Katherine's face was pale, her eyes glassy. "What else do you need?"

"Pillows," Mrs. Havens said calmly. "We need to ensure your friend's comfort."

"Pillows," Katherine repeated, and dashed from the room.

Sarah clutched her stomach as another contraction rocked her. She was drenched in sweat and so terrified the birth was going to go wrong that she wouldn't have noticed if she were laying on pillows or rocks. But she, too, had seen the terror in Katherine's face. If having a purpose would have a calming effect, then Sarah was all for it.

Only one of them could panic, and that person was Sarah.

"Pillows!" Katherine announced as a flock of maids burst into the room, laden with every cushion in the entire townhouse.

"Prop her up," Mrs. Havens ordered, dragging a stool to the foot of the bed. "Knees, too. Won't be long now."

Katherine blanched and began to sway alarmingly.

Mrs. Havens pinned her with a sharp glance. "Your friend is overwarm, Kate. This can be an uncomfortable process. She might like to suck on some ice."

Katherine blinked, then pulled herself together. "Ice. Yes. I can bring ice."

Sarah closed her eyes and groaned as another contraction ripped through her. It was different now, much stronger than her monthly cramps. The pain was sharp, the pressure visceral. It felt like her body was tightening, rather than opening. Like the world's worst constipation. Good Lord, she hoped she didn't make that kind of mess in Katherine's antique bed. Right in front of her.

Sarah's legs ached. Her back ached. Her hips ached. Each new wave was a fresh knife from the top of her stomach through her womb.

By the time Katherine returned with the ice chips, the cramps were coming much faster. Sarah's nightrail was sticky with sweat and she could no longer speak from the fear and the pain.

"What do you need?" Katherine begged. "What can I bring you?"

"Needle and thread in case of tearing," Mrs. Havens said. "Scissors to sever the cord."

"*Edmund*," Sarah managed to pant between another wave of cramps. Panic flooded her. Needles? *Tearing?*

Katherine raced out the door.

"Shh," Mrs. Havens cooed softly, applying gentle pressure on Sarah's knees to widen her thighs. "I'll tell you when to push. So will your body."

Sarah groaned and nodded, no longer embarrassed about her nudity or her fluids. There was too much pain for that. Too much concentration. She just wanted the baby *out*.

Healthy. Safe. And in her arms.

She threw back her head and screamed as the baby's head began to push out into the cool night air.

Mrs. Havens kept up a steady patter of soft, calming words.

Sarah didn't register any of it. She was trying too hard to keep sucking in air, to keep pushing in time with the contractions, to breathe during the pauses, to not cry from exhaustion.

With one last push, the pressure finally eased just as a loud, furious cry rent the air.

Sarah's eyes flew open. *Her baby.* She'd done it!

Her lungs were still too weak to allow for lucid conversation, so she held out her arms and gave Mrs. Havens a tired, relieved smile.

Mrs. Havens quickly bathed the infant with a clean wet cloth before swaddling the tiny limbs and placing the baby in Sarah's waiting arms.

"A boy. Congratulations."

A boy. Tears streamed down her cheeks as Sarah cuddled the baby to her chest. Ruddy cheeks. Bright blue eyes. He was so small, so perfect. Every minute of the birthing was worth it, just to hold him in her arms. Her child.

She *would* make a family for this baby. By force, if necessary. Her son would be the happiest, most well-adjusted boy in the history of children. He would never want for a meal, or doubt his parents' love for him. She would be the best mother that ever lived.

The door flew open and Katherine burst back inside. This time, with Edmund on her heels.

Sarah gazed up at him sleepily. Dreamily. "It's a boy, darling. We have a son."

"We have a son." He fell to his knees beside her, and covered her face with a thousand kisses.

Mrs. Havens turned toward Katherine. "Your friend…"

"*Sarah*, Aunt. This is Sarah."

Mrs. Havens nodded blankly. "Have I met her?"

Edmund's gaze flew to Sarah's in alarm.

She smiled and lifted a shoulder. Nothing mattered but the baby. Her life had completely changed.

"May I hold him?" Edmund's voice was quiet, but eager.

Sarah hesitated. Not because she wished to withhold his son from him, but because she wasn't quite ready to let the baby go. Even for a moment.

"I don't know if—" A sharp pain rocketed through her, stealing her breath. Her head fell back against the pillow in agony. "Take him," she gasped. "Take him."

"What is it?" Edmund stammered, lifting the baby from her arms. "What's wrong?"

Mrs. Havens sat back down on her footstool and grinned at the room. "Your friend is having twins."

CHAPTER 10

In his three years at war, in the long, blood-drenched hours of Waterloo, in the eight arduous months it took to finally make his way home, Brigadier Edmund Blackpool had not once succumbed to panic.

Until now.

His heart banged as he approached his townhouse. He didn't have a baby. He had *two* babies. Two tiny, helpless, completely identical infant sons. Timothy was the one in Sarah's arms. Edmund was holding little Noah.

Probably. Had he mentioned they were completely identical?

Edmund inched up the freshly cleared front walk with slow, careful steps. He did not want his first act as a father to be slipping on an ice patch and flinging his newborn baby into the sky.

London wasn't helping matters. The babies were as displeased with the noise and the crowds as Edmund was, although their red-faced cries were much louder. The stink of the waste and the layer of soot from a city of burning coal were as unpleasant for the babies as the bitter wind and the blinding yellow sun.

His first goal was to get them tucked away inside as quickly and safely as possible.

His second goal was to figure out what the devil to do next.

The cradle was a good size, but was it large enough for two babies? Or would they have to keep one in their arms while the other one slept until Edmund could get an additional cradle delivered?

Presuming the babies would ever sleep. Or that Sarah would allow them to leave her arms. So far Edmund hadn't seen much evidence of either possibility.

As soon as they drew near the front step, the footman swung open the door and ushered them inside. Edmund and Sarah stared at each other for a long moment as the cozy interior warmth replaced the chill of the city.

There. Now they were inside. With their coats and scarves and hats and boots and winter gloves still on.

Holding two tiny babies.

"Er," said Edmund.

Sarah raised her brows in question.

He smiled awkwardly and wished he hadn't said anything. Sweat dripped down his spine.

Edmund had earned the title of brigadier because of his skill at organizing and deploying soldiers. He *wasn't* good at developing a winning battle plan that encompassed an exhausted bride, married life, and two infant children.

His blood boiled in frustration. He hated not knowing what to do. All his dreams—romantic waltzes, long walks along the river, fireworks under the stars—had disappeared the moment Sarah was actually within his sight.

He'd wanted this to be perfect. He'd wanted to *be* perfect. He longed to have her look at him again the way she used to do before. When she'd thought he was magnificent and capable of anything. When she'd loved him.

Instead, they were slowly sweating to death in the middle of his austere bachelor townhouse.

Which Sarah had never before seen. Edmund straightened. *That* was something he could do!

"Come," he said gruffly. "Let me show you your new home."

She followed him through the parlor to the dining room, around the kitchen and up the stairway to the master bedroom, and the nursery that had once been his study.

He stopped there because it seemed the most practical place to pause, and tilted his head toward the singular cradle. "I sent for another before we left Miss Ross's house. It may take a day or two, but—"

"It's lovely," Sarah said tiredly, as if she barely registered his presence at all. "Thank you."

He was appalled at his lack of insight. "You're exhausted. Of course you're exhausted. Let's… let's do something. Would you like to lie down? I can… er… watch the babies…"

By himself. Alone. Dear God, what was he saying?

"They're hungry," Sarah said, gazing down at the one in her arms. Timothy. Most likely. "That's why they're fussing. And my breasts ache. I think I'm leaking milk inside my coat."

Her breasts ached. Leaking milk. He had to take action. Edmund glanced around the room in search of inspiration.

"Put Timothy inside the cradle, and take off your coat and gloves. Then you can feed him."

"Noah."

"Er, Noah. Put Noah in the cradle."

When Sarah met his gaze, her eyes were laughing. "Do you have any idea which is which?"

"Do you?" Edmund countered brilliantly. He wasn't certain which way he hoped she'd answer.

"I do, actually. You're holding Noah—"

"I knew it!" The back of his neck heated at her raised brow. He flashed a guilty smile. "Or, at least, I suspected strongly."

"—and I am holding Timothy."

"How can you be certain?"

"Their hair."

Edmund cast a skeptical glance at the wiggling baby in his arms. "They both have precisely one tuft of hair."

"Look closer." Sarah stepped closer. "Noah's whorl of hair curls off to the right, whilst Timothy's cowlick curves off to the left."

Edmund stared at both babies, then grinned at Sarah. "You're a bloody genius."

Her smile vanished as though he'd slapped her.

"No profanity in front of the babies," she hissed.

He blinked. "They're one day old. They have no idea what we're saying."

Her jaw set. "It's a bad habit, and we're not going to do it."

Fine. Edmund clamped his teeth together to keep from responding. No swearing in front of infants. If that was the line he needed to walk to get her to look at him like she used to, so be it.

He gestured across the room with his elbow. "Please put Timothy in the cradle and take off your coat. I don't want you to get overheated. The babies' safety and your comfort are my sole priorities."

The moment Sarah laid Timothy in the cradle, he started screaming. She snatched him right back up and his cries immediately ceased.

"Put him down," Edmund repeated.

"I can't," Sarah said wretchedly. "He'll cry."

Edmund narrowed his eyes. One day old, and his son had already mastered the art of manipulating women. "You can't feed him if you're wearing seven layers of clothing and *I* can't feed him no matter what I do. You're going to have to put him down. Long enough to take off your coat, at least."

She stared at the cradle doubtfully. "I'll have to unlace my gown."

"And unlace your gown," Edmund agreed. Sarah had mentioned she hadn't bothered with stays since about the third month of her pregnancy, but there was still a shift and a morning dress between her breast and her child.

Sarah took a deep breath and placed Timothy back into the cradle. He screamed as if it were a vat of lava. She shot a pleading glance toward Edmund.

He shook his head firmly. "Coat."

She shucked out of her coat and tossed it against the wall, then froze in horror. "I can't reach the buttons on my back."

Timothy's cries grew more insistent.

"Ring the bell pull," Edmund said patiently. "We can get help."

Sarah shook her head. "I don't want your servants to see my breasts."

"The housekeeper—"

"Will not see me leaking milk from my nipples!" Her voice cracked in desperation.

"Hold Noah." Edmund transferred the baby to her

arms. Timothy seemed to wail louder at the slight. Edmund slipped off his coat, hat, gloves, scarf, and threw everything in the corner atop Sarah's. He loosened Sarah's gown from neck to waist, then rushed over to the cradle to pick up his screaming son.

Timothy quieted the moment he was in his father's arms and Edmund smiled.

"What are you doing?" Sarah demanded.

He eased into one of the rocking chairs. "Letting you feed Noah."

"But Timothy was crying first."

"He's not crying now, and you're holding Noah. Is there honestly a reason to switch?" Edmund stopped rocking in order to glance over at his suspiciously silent wife.

Her eyes were welling with tears.

"Bloody hell," he muttered, leaping to his feet.

At his blatant lapse in the no-profanity rule, tears spilled down her cheeks. Devil take it.

He laid Timothy in the cradle, and was rewarded with the baby's immediate ear-splitting cries. He plucked Noah from Sarah's arms and jerked his head toward the cradle. "There. Now you can feed Timothy. He's even crying again."

Sarah covered her face with her hands and choked back a sob.

"I don't *know* what order to do things in," she said miserably, and turned toward the cradle. "I just want to be a good mother. I'm doing everything wrong."

"You're a wonderful mother," he assured her as she picked up the crying baby. "Look at me. I have no idea what's happening, either. We'll figure it out together."

Sarah sniffed back her tears and sank into the other rocking chair. She pulled down her bodice and lifted Timothy to her chest.

Edmund closed his eyes in relief.

"It's not working," Sarah cried desperately. "He's not sucking."

"Maybe he's not hungry."

"He hasn't *eaten*."

Edmund tilted his head. "Maybe he's nervous."

"Maybe it's me," she said, her expression bordering on panic. "Maybe there's something wrong with my nipples and my children are going to die of starvation because I can't even feed them!"

"It's not that," he assured her.

"Then what is it?" she asked, her eyes wide.

Edmund swallowed. Truth be told, he had absolutely no idea.

All Sarah wanted was to be a good mother. Well, all he wanted was to be a good husband and father.

Thus far, it wasn't going very well.

Putting aside the fact that she'd run away within minutes of saying their vows rather than spend another moment in his company, his wife's eyes were purple with exhaustion, she winced every time she moved, and the babe whose mouth was pressed to her leaking nipple was refusing to suckle.

She wasn't just completely in her rights to be half-hysterical.

Sarah was counting on Edmund to fix the problem.

"Try Noah," he said.

Her lips tightened. "Edmund…"

"Maybe Timothy *isn't* hungry. Or maybe he doesn't know what to do either. But it's not working, so there's nothing to lose by giving Noah a shot."

She bit her lip. "Alright."

He placed Noah into the cradle, then took Timothy from Sarah so she could push to her feet and rescue the now-sobbing Noah.

She sat back down and brought the baby to her breast.

Noah immediately began to suckle.

Relief flooded through Edmund as he sagged back into the rocking chair with Timothy. "There. He's doing it. Do you feel better?"

Sarah stared at him with startled, pleading eyes. "It *hurts*."

Bloody hell. Edmund stared back at her in silence and frustration. He wanted this to *work*. All of it. Life. Parenthood. Marriage.

So far, there was plenty of room for improvement.

He couldn't escape the irony. Once the babies learned to feed and Sarah got some rest... then what? When he'd dreamed of the moment he saw Sarah's naked breast again, he certainly hadn't anticipated this. She was so fragile, so wounded. He couldn't begin to imagine what he'd put her through. The pregnancy. The delivery. He wouldn't blame her if she never wished to make love to him again. A good husband would give her all the space she required.

Edmund was scared to touch her, for fear of hurting her. He was suffused with guilt at the droop in her spine, the dark blotches beneath her eyes. This entire situation was his fault.

He would never hurt her again.

CHAPTER 11

A week later, Sarah scooted her chair closer to the fireplace and retrieved her sewing basket from the carpet.

The twins were asleep—for the moment—which meant now was as good a time as any to try and salvage what she could of her two most comfortable morning dresses. Her eyes were so tired she could barely keep them open, but she could not sleep while there was work to be done.

She piled the material atop her knees. The armless chairs required her to wrestle the fabric in her lap to keep it from slipping to the floor, but she had no alternative. Some sort of finance fellow had come calling for Edmund, and since he no longer had a study in which to receive business callers, the small downstairs sitting room was the only choice.

Finances. Sarah stabbed her pins into the faded cloth. Whenever a money man had come to the Fairfax home, it had either been to evict them for unpaid rents or to threaten violence upon her brother for his gambling debts.

Her fingers trembled as she pulled her shears from the basket and began slicing the bodice off the dress in her lap. Whatever horror she'd had of revisiting the poorest moments of her youth had tripled now that she had the welfare of an entire family to worry about.

They needed to stay in London—the city was rich with opportunities for two growing boys—but moving in with her parents was not an option. Their household was smaller, and an even less stable environment. Edmund's brother Bartholomew was rock solid, but had no room for yet another newly married couple and their infant twins.

She would have to ask Ravenwood for money. Edmund would hate taking charity from the man who'd almost taken his bride, but it was the only way. She would not risk her family's health, her children's lives. Sarah set down her shears. If begging for alms was the sole solution, then she would waste no time in—

"What are you doing?"

She jerked her head over her shoulder. Edmund stood in the open doorway. "How was your meeting?"

He stepped toward her, his brow furrowing in confusion. "Are you cutting up your dresses?"

She curled her shaking hands into fists. "Are we being evicted?"

He pulled up short. "What?"

"Our finances," she gritted out. "How bad is it?"

"Neither good nor bad. But I'm working on it. Danbury and I were discussing some investments I'd made."

Investments? With what capital? A horrible thought made her dizzy with fear. "Are you gambling?"

"Look at me." He lifted her chin in his hand. "I am

not gambling. We will not be evicted. Nothing is wrong."

She jerked her chin from his grasp. He was wrong. Investing *was* gambling. It meant tying up money the family might need now. It meant the possibility of losing it all in the future. "What kind of investments?"

He lifted one of the limp sleeves in her lap. "Why are you cutting up your gowns?"

"Because I'm trying to be practical." Her eyes stung at the idea of losing hope for stability. "Someone has to."

"How is ruining dresses practical?"

"They're already ruined. This bodice is stretched and stained beyond all salvation." She lifted the one on her lap, then gestured toward the sewing basket. "And the skirt of that one has been re-hemmed so many times it's fraying at the seams. By combining the usable parts of each, I can create a serviceable day dress."

Edmund eyed the material doubtfully. "With a purple muslin bodice and an orange and yellow cotton print skirt?"

"I didn't say it would be beautiful." She tossed the dress aside and leapt up to glare at him. "I said it would be *usable*."

He gripped her shoulders and lowered his face toward hers. "I want it to be beautiful. I want you to *feel* beautiful."

"I don't want to feel beautiful." Her lip trembled as she gazed up at him. "I want to *be* beautiful."

"You are," he said quietly.

Liar. Her throat tightened. They both knew she was not.

She tore her gaze away so he wouldn't see the hurt in her eyes. She couldn't hide from the truth.

Her post-pregnancy body was even less attractive than her pregnant body. A feat she hadn't thought possible. She could scarcely stand to see herself naked, but Edmund had been avoiding her touch even fully clothed. A far cry from the man who nine months ago couldn't keep his hands away from her.

Nor had she wished him to. If she'd had any idea their intimacy then would lead to such a chasm today...

"Those dresses are rags." He lifted her chin with his knuckle. "Let me buy you a new gown. We can commission an entire—"

"I don't want a new gown." She forced her eyes to meet his. "I want a home I'll never have to leave. A husband who will never leave me. A happy, healthy family, with—"

"I will *never* leave you," he growled, gripping her shoulders. "I did not walk one hundred miles and sail two hundred more just to give you up. If you prefer hideous patchwork gowns, wear them. But for as long as I am alive, you will have a home and you will have me."

She stared up at hm. His gaze was hot and unwavering. His body mere inches from hers. She trembled, her entire body thrilling to finally, *finally*, be back in his arms. If he were not gripping her so tightly, she could lean forward just enough to brush her breasts against his strong chest.

Perhaps if she touched him, he would remember how much he had loved to touch her. Perhaps if she closed her eyes to concentrate solely on the feel of his body next to hers, the past would melt away. Perhaps if he kissed her, if he touched her, she could believe he still found her desirable.

Pulse pounding, she reached for him with hopeful, hesitant fingers. If they could kiss, if they could at least *embrace*—

The moment her hands brushed his waistcoat, he jerked away as if scalded by her touch.

He released her shoulders and leapt backward, running a hand through his hair as though to rid his palm of the feel of her body.

Her heart broke. She slumped back down onto the chair and retrieved the fallen day dress. "Go mind your investments, then. I'll take care of the mending."

"I can commission—"

"*Go*," she repeated without looking up. If he could not bear to touch her, then no gown on earth would make her feel beautiful. She would concentrate on being practical. On nurturing the twins. On resigning herself to a life without passion.

She kept her eyes on her sewing. She would make it through this. One stitch at a time.

CHAPTER 12

Within weeks of giving birth, Sarah could feed her newborn babies in her sleep. In fact, she was pretty certain that was precisely what was happening most of the time. She lived in a constant state of exhaustion.

Sarah eased into a rocking chair to burp the baby. She was so tired. When was the last time she'd slept soundly? Long before the twins. Before discovering she was with child. Before learning Edmund was presumed dead. She hadn't had a restful night's sleep since the day he'd purchased a commission in the Army.

Now he was back. A miracle. A nightmare.

Had she worried her husband's interest would wane now that her bright eyes and slender figure had been replaced by heavy purple bags and a flabby, sagging stomach? A harsh laugh strangled in her throat.

His interest hadn't simply *waned*. Edmund flinched if he so much as touched her.

Oh, he was a model husband. A model father. He was up with the babies just as often as she was, and did everything in his power to ensure she had every comfort. Favorite foods. Soft pillows. Expensive robes.

They argued. Fiercely. He'd wanted to employ a wet nurse, a nanny. Despite the much-needed relief such help would bring, she could not allow him to whittle away what little resources they had on tasks she could do herself. She'd spent four-and-twenty years watching her parents piddle away the slightest fortune in the blink of an eye. She would not repeat their mistakes.

Would she repeat her own?

Sarah gazed down at the nursing babe in her arms. Love filled her heart. She didn't regret having children. Nor did she regret the actions that led to her pregnancy. She wished their moments of passion hadn't been limited to one night.

It wasn't just that she needed Edmund to desire her still. She wanted to *deserve* his desire. And she knew she didn't. Couldn't begin to try.

Where she had once been pretty enough to catch any man's eye, a glimpse of her own reflection was like peering at a stranger. A pale, fat, flabby, exhausted stranger. No wonder Edmund recoiled from the slightest physical contact. She could barely stand the sight of her own skin when bathing herself. If she hated her body, why should her husband feel any different?

The nursery door creaked open. Soft candlelight from wall sconces in the corridor outlined her husband's wide shoulders and tousled head.

"Why didn't you wake me?"

"I had to feed the twins. That's not something you're equipped to help with."

He entered the nursery and sank into the rocking chair next to hers. "You don't have to do it alone."

Sarah didn't reply. There was no point in telling

him she felt more alone than ever when he was inches away but still miles out of reach. But what was the alternative?

The only thing worse than no longer being desirable would be forcing him to feign his attraction.

She'd never had to feign hers.

His eyes looked just as sleep-deprived as hers, but it didn't matter. She found him as irresistible as the day they'd met. He had changed, too, but the hardness in his muscles, the darkness in his eyes, somehow made him even more dangerously attractive.

He wasn't just stronger than before. The piercing intensity in his eyes, the constant readiness in his stance enveloped him with an aura of coiled power. When all that singleminded focus was pointed at her, Sarah's knees melted. She forced herself to look away.

'Twasn't just that she yearned to feel his touch. She feared it. Dreaded the moment his firm hands gripped her waist—and discovered it now squished like pudding.

Her throat tightened. She was no longer the woman he'd left. The one thing that surpassed her desire for her husband was the terror of rejection. She agonized about the day Edmund would finally reach for her… only to be repulsed by what he found.

She wasn't his dream woman anymore. She was over-tired, hyper-sensitive, stretched-out reality.

Sarah pushed to her feet and lay little Timothy back in his cradle. With any luck, perhaps she could steal another hour's sleep.

She turned from the cradle and gasped to find Edmund towering just behind her. She hadn't heard him rise from his chair. And now she was trapped between the sleeping babies in their cradles and the immovable wall of her husband's chest. Her heart thundered as she lifted her gaze to his.

"Are you avoiding me?" His eyes were dark. Furious.

She kept her voice steady. "How could I avoid you? I live in your house. Sleep in your bed."

When she slept at all. She'd once imagined married life would mean the sensual exhaustion of nights spent lovemaking. Not the delirious fatigue of taking care of twins, of falling into bed half-conscious, only to lie awake searching for a position that didn't hurt her back or make her nipples leak.

Or bring her into contact with her husband.

So, yes. She was avoiding him. Or had been. There was nowhere to go but backwards into the cradles or forward into his arms.

She held her ground.

"Are you angry with me?" His eyes were dark, his voice deceptively light. "Is that the problem? You see me as a villain in all of this?"

Of course she wasn't angry with him . She was bitter at the entire situation. For both of them. His homecoming should've been a dream come true. Their wedding, a fairy story. Their lives full of pleasure. Surely he felt the same.

"Do you see me as a villainess?" she snapped back.

He blinked in confusion. "You?"

She gestured toward her belly. "Me."

He shook his head. "Bruges was more my fault than yours. I do not blame you for becoming pregnant."

His words were carefully chosen.

She was not fooled. Her eyes narrowed. "What, precisely, *do* you blame me for?"

"I'm not angry at you." His lips tightened. "I'm

angry at everyone. At myself. I thought I was invincible." He clenched his fingers. "I was wrong."

She bit her lip.

"I thought my friends would never leave me. I was wrong." His eyes flashed with hurt. "I thought I would be searched for, missed, rescued. I was wrong."

Her heart twisted.

"I thought I would come home to you, to the life we used to have." He clenched his jaw. "I was wrong." His smile was bitter. "You cannot expect me not to be... disillusioned."

She wrapped her arms about her stomach, hurt mixing with fury. "You have suffered. But you are not the only one who has faced challenges and disappointment. You can't reappear after nearly a year and expect everything to be just as it was!"

His lip curled. "You tried to marry my childhood friend and give his name to my sons. They would have never known that I—"

"Did you expect me to wait on a *dead* man?" she exploded.

"I may be dead inside, but I'm more than alive enough for you." He gripped her chin and covered her mouth with his.

Desire ripped through her like brushfire, lighting every nerve from the inside out. His teeth on her lips, his hands in her hair, his mouth claiming hers—*this* was what she had wanted. What she had feared. What she desperately needed.

Her tongue met his. Sparring. Mating. She reached for him, drowning in the delight of soft linen over hard muscle.

His body was hot to the touch. Strange and familiar. He tasted like Edmund, smelled like Edmund, felt like second chances. He kissed her as if she were as indispensable as air. As though his every heartbeat belonged as much to her as it did to him.

She'd lost a part of herself when she'd thought he'd died. Having him back was marvelous, but having his lips on hers was like having life again. She was no longer tired, but electrified. Her body thrummed with yearning, with anticipation, with desire. She wanted more than kisses—she wanted *him*.

His fingers reached for her waist. Not her waist. Her soft, loose flesh.

She jerked away instinctively.

He released her at once, leaping backward as if she were a grenade whose detonation would destroy them both.

Perhaps she was.

"My apologies," he said, his voice as stiff as his posture. "I lost my head. It shall not be repeated."

That's what she was afraid of.

She turned her back so that she would not have to see him walk away.

CHAPTER 13

A fortnight later, Edmund was still cursing the moment of weakness, the moment of intense *want*, that had made him crush his lips to his wife's. She had obviously been far from ready. He had vowed not to pressure her. To never make her feel hunted or frightened.

And now she was more skittish than ever.

He tried to give her space to heal, to get used to having a husband and children. She was adamant against hiring nannies or wet nurses, which was why he spent an hour every afternoon in the nursery, up to his elbows in baby bathwater while Sarah caught a few moments' sleep.

Despite her subtly disapproving frowns, the housekeeper always lent a capable hand—*she*, at least, saw the value in a live-in nanny—and Edmund had come to cherish these moments spent with his sons.

He wanted to be useful. To be needed.

He was neither.

Edmund had not birthed the babies. He could not nurse them. His wife did not want for his assistance. Bathing them was something Edmund could do. Helping whenever possible was how he could be a good father to his children, a good husband to his wife. To buy her an hour's peace before it was time for feedings all over again. These were the moments when he felt things had perhaps worked out exactly as they were supposed to.

Until today.

Yesterday, the housekeeper had left for Leeds. Mrs. Clark hadn't had a spare moment since Edmund had returned home, so when one of her parents had fallen ill, he could scarcely demand she eschew familial obligations in favor of helping a brigadier bathe a pair of twins. She would return in less than a week's time. Edmund would simply have to handle things in the meantime.

It wasn't going well.

The twins had been awake (and their mother asleep) when Edmund had first sent for the tub and warm water. The footman had fetched everything upstairs with his usual alacrity, yet the twins had still managed to fall asleep before they could be bathed.

Unless they'd learned to playact.

Edmund hated to wake them—the ornery devils were quite angelic in slumber—but Sarah never napped for long. This was his sole opportunity to ease her load.

So he'd inched over to the cradle and began to undress Noah.

Upon doing so, Timothy immediately started to shrill from the other cradle, giving credence to the idea that they had known Edmund was there all along and simply had no wish to be clean and bathed.

Edmund set down Noah and started with Timothy instead, which unfortunately served to set both boys howling. He strode over to the tub and lowered the protesting infant's feet into basin, only to get a snootful of cold, soapy water splashed directly into his face.

The water had cooled while his imps had feigned sleep. Naturally.

He shook the suds from his hair and carried Timothy—now gurgling with delight—back to his cradle so Edmund could ring the footman for a bucket of hot water.

In the meantime, Edmund yanked off his cravat, his pocket watch, his waistcoat. If his sons intended to fight dirty, a soldier ought to be prepared. He crossed his arms over his waist and hiked his bath-splattered linen shirt up and over his head.

"What on Earth is happening in here?"

Edmund whirled about to see his wife standing in the open doorway. "I…"

"What *happened?*" she repeated in horror. This time, she was not looking at his discarded clothing, but rather the network of corded scars crisscrossing his chest and arms.

He put his shirt back on. "Waterloo."

Her lip trembled. "Edmund—"

"Fresh water," called the footman as he heaved two steaming buckets into the nursery. "Quite hot."

Edmund pulled Sarah to his side.

After the footman dumped the first bucket into the tub, Edmund stopped him in order to test the water. He didn't want it cold, but nor did he want it scalding. "Leave the extra bucket. We may have use for it later."

The footman nodded and quit the nursery.

Sarah turned to Edmund and placed her fingertips to his chest. "Your scars…"

"We should hurry," he said roughly. "Let's get our sons bathed and back into their warm clothes."

It was the right choice. The only choice. And yet

his entire traitorous body felt bereft when her warm fingers lifted from his chest as she turned away.

"Will they both fit into the tub at the same time?" she asked as she moved toward Noah's cradle.

He glanced at the tub. It was certainly large enough for two small infants. "Mrs. Clark and I usually do one at a time."

Come to think of it, Edmund had no idea why. It would seem more efficient to bathe both at once, and be done faster. No need to muck with water temperature and the like.

"You take Noah," he said. "I'll grab Timothy."

She began to push the baby's blanket aside, then shot a startled look at Edmund. "Where are his clothes?"

Edmund's neck heated.. "I was going to bathe him, but he'd fallen asleep and then the water grew chill… We should hasten, so the same doesn't happen anew."

He pushed up his sleeves and turned to the other cradle. Timothy blinked up at him innocently. A smile curved Edmund's lips. "Your mother is joining us for baths today, so none of your tricks, little man."

The moment he unwrapped the blankets swaddling his naked son, Edmund covered the baby's naked middle with a clean, folded cloth—which Timothy immediately soaked with warm urine.

"*Ha*. Caught you." Edmund tossed the soiled cloth onto a waiting towel in the corner. He lifted Timothy into his arms and turned toward Sarah—just in time to see Noah let loose over the cradle with an impressive arc of baby piss.

Sarah leapt backward just as Edmund darted forward with another square of clean, folded cloth to block the flow. In seconds, it was over.

She turned to him with wide, shocked eyes. "Why did he…"

His lips twitched. No coarse language in front of the infants limited the ability to discuss the fountain of baby piss that had just arced halfway across the room.

"'Twasn't you, darling. It's one of their favorite bath-time games. Something about the cool air on their naked… berries," he substituted at the last second.

Sarah's cheeks turned red with embarrassment for only a moment before she bit back a giggle and cast a suspicious eye on the cradle. "Is he going to do it again?"

"Not if we make haste."

Grinning, Edmund carried Timothy over to the tub and knelt to the floor. Now that the babies were almost six weeks old, their heads no longer wobbled unsteadily as they'd done when first born. Nonetheless, Edmund was careful to support the back of Timothy's neck until the baby was safely propped on the floor of the tub.

Clear warm water lapped at the baby's bare chest. Timothy's chubby little hands slapped at the surface as he gurgled happily.

Edmund's smile softened as Sarah knelt on the other side in order to gently place Noah in the opposite end of the basin. Edmund's gaze softened. Earlier, he had believed that there was nothing better than the pride of doing something helpful for his wife whilst enabling her to snatch some much-deserved sleep. He enjoyed the time spent with his sons.

As it happened, he enjoyed spending time with his sons and his wife together even more.

"Do I have piddle in my hair?" she whispered, her

eyes sparkling with laughter above her flushed cheeks.

"Not much," he assured her with a straight face. "You look almost becoming."

She flicked water at him. "Rogue. You look like a disheveled mess."

"Thank you," he said solemnly. "Decades from now, when our children ask how I fell in love with their mother, I'll say 'twas her sweet, gentle compliments during bath-time, and her fleetness of foot whilst dodging a flow of—"

She burst out laughing and began to soap Noah. "I suspect the three of you will keep me quite entertained for the rest of my life."

Edmund's stomach sank. Rather than reply, he concentrated on washing Timothy.

As he had learned so acutely, the rest of their lives was something that could not be counted upon. Perhaps they would live to be eighty. Or perhaps the entire family would contract smallpox upon the morrow. He no longer had faith in the next year, in the next sunrise. The future was uncertain and unpromised. He would enjoy this moment, every moment, spent with Sarah and his sons. Every minute was a gift to be cherished. While it lasted.

In moments like these, with his wrinkled linen shirt streaked with bathwater and his wife's twinkling eyes meeting his over a tub full of two wiggling infants, he couldn't help but believe he was the most fortunate man alive.

Unfortunately, the bathwater would not stay warm forever, so he lifted Timothy from the tub as soon as he was clean. Edmund wrapped his son in a towel before carrying him to his cradle to be changed into a fresh gown. The baby would sleep peacefully.

His eyelids were already drowsing as Edmund tucked the blanket about him.

He turned at the sound of wet bubbles and his wife's snickers.

"It's Noah," she said as if trying not to giggle. "He made wind in the water and was so startled, his eyes just—"

"Get him *out*. Get him out!" Edmund raced over to the tub just as a cloud of mustard color spread from behind the baby's legs and instantly saturated the entire basin.

Sarah froze in place, a strangled cry emanating from her pallid throat. What had once been clean bathwater was now a clotted cloud of yellow-orange muck, lapping at her fingers and the baby's chest like waves at a putrid shore. The blood drained from her face as she scrambled to her feet to hold her dripping, gurgling infant well above the soiled tub below.

Edmund raced forward with a clean towel spread wide in a flag of surrender just in time to block flying droplets as his infant son began to kick and gurgle with glee.

"We cannot just dry him off," said Sarah as she relinquished the dripping baby to Edmund. "He needs to be bathed anew." She glanced down at her wet fingers. "As do I."

"I'll be quick." Edmund knelt between the tub and the last bucket of water the footman had left in the nursery. Steam no longer rose from the water inside, but it was clean and that was all that mattered.

He lay his swaddled baby upon an unfolded towel. This time, he did not place the child anywhere near the water, but instead dipped the corners of a fresh towel into the last bucket and rewashed his son from the torso down.

Noah having already done his business, the

process went quickly. In no time, Edmund scooped him back up to return him to his cradle.

While Edmund ensured both infants were in their sleeping gowns and tucked in safe and warm, Sarah was over at the bucket, scrubbing her hands with the last of the clean water.

Noah's eyes drowsed. Timothy was already fast asleep. The excitement had ended.

Edmund sank heavily into a rocking chair and rested his head against the curved wooden back. Sarah eased into the rocking chair next to him, her face still pale, but the corners of her mouth twitching.

She glanced around the nursery—empty bucket, dirty tub, discarded waistcoat, mountains of used cloths, waterlogged parents, sleeping infants—and met Edmund's eyes.

They both burst out laughing.

He leaned forward to steal a quick kiss from her smiling mouth before taking her hand in his and leaning back against his chair to rock in exhausted silence, hand-in-hand with his wife.

"We're doing fine, aren't we?" Her soft question did not sound worried, but rather slightly mystified. As if not until this very moment had she had a moment to reflect on how different their lives had become—and how well they had adapted to the new changes.

He squeezed her hand. "We're better than fine. We're a family."

It was true. Peace spread through his tired body. They *were* a family.

"We almost weren't," Sarah said quietly, her eyes downcast. "Not just because of Waterloo. Because of me. Because I was going to marry—"

He stopped rocking to look her in the eyes. "You

were the commander of your own war. Sometimes the hard choice is the right choice. I shall never blame you for doing everything within your power to ensure the safety of our children."

She bit her lip. "About Ravenwood…"

A flash of jealousy bit through him. Edmund pulled her onto his lap before she could finish whatever she'd been about to say. "I don't care about Ravenwood. You both did what you thought was right, in the circumstances that you were given." He cupped her cheek with his hand. "I don't care about the past. It's over."

She nodded and lay her head against his shoulder. Despite the events of the afternoon, her soft brown hair still carried the scent of her subtle perfume.

"How can you not care about the past?" she asked quietly. "It's all I ever think about. That, and how I'm going to manage the future."

His eyes closed. "The only thing that matters is that we have each other now."

He pressed a kiss to the top of her head and wrapped his arms about his wife.

At last, he felt like he'd come home.

CHAPTER 14

The following morning at the breakfast table, Edmund's wife brought up the one topic he most wished to avoid.

The Duke of Ravenwood.

"We don't need to talk about it," he said again, hoping to stop her before she listed the many obvious ways a marriage to Ravenwood would have been an improvement over her current situation. Edmund had just started feeling like he had a family again. A future. He didn't want to think about what he might have taken from Sarah to get them there.

"You don't have to talk about it." She set down her teacup and saucer. "But I do think you should listen."

Edmund's stomach soured. He might love Sarah until his last breath, but his devotion couldn't purchase sprawling estates and retinues of maids, footmen, modistes, nannies, and governesses in a number large enough to rival an army. He couldn't give her that. All he could give her was himself.

He pushed his plate away. "Say what you think you need to say."

She took a deep breath. "I was desperate—"

"I know you were desperate. I never meant—"

"You're not letting me talk." She clasped her hands together and regarded them for a long moment.

He did his best not to interrupt. Or to wish his tea was brandy.

"The day you died, I died too." Her gaze lifted and met his. "You were everything to me. My heart. My hope. The world that I loved was now bleak. It seemed there was little to live for. And then I missed my first menses."

His muscles flinched. He could not imagine what that must have been like. He wasn't sure he wanted to find out.

"Joy," she said softly. "*Terror*. I still had a part of you... but what was I to do now? You were dead. I was on my own—but not for long. The sands were slipping through the hourglass faster than I could catch them. In a scant nine months, I would bear a child. But my belly would betray my condition even faster. I did not have the two things I needed most... You, and time."

He shifted uncomfortably. Being left for dead was not his fault. But he was absolutely to blame for not taking obvious precautions whilst debauching his betrothed.

That night in Bruges... He had missed her for so long. Wanted her so badly he could barely think about anything other than making her his. His blood had raced every time he so much as thought her name.

Much like now. He couldn't even sit across from her at a breakfast table without thinking about the scent of her skin, the soft silk of her hair. He dreamed every night about the taste of her kisses, the sound of her breath catching as he plunged himself into her hot, tight—

He gripped the edges of his chair and forced his

clattering heart to slow. *This* was how he'd ruined everything in Bruges. He would not allow his ardor to ruin their marriage. Sarah needed time, not passionate advances. For all that was holy, his wife was still thinking about *Ravenwood*.

She had chosen Edmund. He had to make certain she didn't regret it.

Starting with letting her tell her story.

"Whose idea was it?" he blurted, then immediately ground his teeth together. He didn't want to know. She was his now. The past was over.

Her voice shook. "My parents wanted me to slip away to the country and give the baby to a nice orphanage."

Rage raced through his body like a lit fuse. The thought of his children growing up parentless in an orphanage... But what options had she had? She had no fortune of her own. No means to support her child. And no man would wed a pregnant bride.

No one except Ravenwood.

"My brother opened an account for me that same day, to do with as I would. I now have a small bit of money." Her cheeks flushed. "That is, *we* now have a small bit of money. It's for all of us, in case of emergency. I hope never to have to use it." She bit her lip. "I was terrified I might have to."

His fingers dug into his palms. He kept them out of sight beneath the table.

"Oliver came to me first," she continued. "He didn't have a ha'penny to his name, but you know how he is. One look at my belly and it was clear I needed rescuing."

Edmund's lips twisted into a smile. He knew exactly how his friends were. Good men. Every last bloody one of them. Of course they would have done their best to help Sarah.

"Realistically," she continued. "Ravenwood was the only choice. Bartholomew hadn't left his bedchamber since returning from war, and Xavier had only recently started talking again…"

Edmund blinked at her. "Xavier wasn't talking?"

She shook her head. "He looked whole. But he came home more damaged than the rest."

Edmund's chest tightened. He had missed so much while he was gone. He hadn't been there for anyone. Not Sarah. Not his brother. Not his friends. Yet all of them had managed to find their own way out of the darkness. Perhaps they hadn't experienced what Edmund had gone through, but they'd each been mired in a hell of their own.

"It was Ravenwood's idea," she said at last, her voice little more than a sigh. "I fought it at first. I felt like I was betraying you."

"I was dead," Edmund said.

"I was betraying your memory. Our love. I was betraying your entire family. Robbing your parents of their grandchild. Forcing an heir upon Ravenwood. The title would have passed to a child that wasn't even his blood."

Edmund swallowed. That… was true. He hadn't thought about what it meant for Ravenwood. He hadn't been stealing Edmund's bride. He'd been destroying his hopes for his own future. Someone else's child would have inherited the dukedom his family had built up for generations. Ravenwood wasn't just rescuing Sarah. He'd been sacrificing himself for Edmund.

For friendship.

He stood up from the table and pulled Sarah into his arms. She wrapped her arms about him and buried her head on his chest. He stroked her hair, kissed her temple. Held her close.

"You did the best that you could," he said quietly. "You thought I was dead."

"You *weren't* dead."

"You didn't know that." He laid his cheek to her hair and inhaled deeply.

She shuddered. "I betrayed you."

"You didn't." He stroked her cheek. "I'm here, Sarah. You're safe. I'm back. Feel my arms about you. My heartbeat against yours. I have you now." He pressed a kiss to her hair. "And I will never let you go."

CHAPTER 15

A week later, Sarah stood before the sitting room window and gazed outside. She lifted a freshly poured cup of tea to her lips and inhaled the steamy aroma.

May. 'Twas already the end of May. The bustling street was awash with sunshine and the sounds of city life. Her eyes crinkled. Jaunty curricles clopped past vendors peddling fresh-picked flowers or piping-hot pies. Children's laughter mixed with the chirping of birds. The twins were eight weeks old. Soon they would be old enough to take to parks. To play with other children.

She set down her teacup to crack open the window. A cool breeze ruffled her hair and brought a smile to her lips. She closed her eyes. On days like this, she longed to be out-of-doors. To spread her arms wide. To tilt her face up toward the sun and breathe in the smell of springtime.

The window slammed down.

She started, her eyes flying open in surprise. Her breath caught. She was no longer alone in the sitting room. Edmund had joined her.

He edged her out of the way in order to yank the curtains closed. His hands trembled.

She touched her fingers to his arm. "I am sorry. Is the air too cold?"

"The city is too... *city*." He stepped back from the hidden pane as though stray carriage wheels might tumble in at any moment.

Sarah bit her lip. "I'm sorry—"

"Do not apologize. You have never been the problem. It's nothing." He ran a hand through his hair and motioned across the room toward the tea table. "May I freshen your cup?"

Her eyes narrowed as she took in Edmund and his townhouse from a fresh perspective. Putting aside the inherent *let's-not-discuss-it* suspiciousness of her big, rugged brigadier offering to pour tea, she couldn't help but notice that the chairs and tables of the sitting room were placed as far as possible from any windows or points of entry.

In fact, none of the rooms in his townhouse had sofas or chairs near any windows. Some had pieces of furniture before the sills, making opening the curtains inconvenient at best. In here, they were well protected from the outside world.

She took Edmund's arm and allowed him to lead her back to the sofa.

Until today, she hadn't thought much about the lack of natural sunlight in the townhouse. To be honest, she'd been incapable of much thought at all—two newborn babies needed constant nurturing, and didn't leave much time for reflecting on one's greater environment.

That, and, in her exhaustion, dim candlelit rooms had been perfect for her tired eyes.

Her heart thudded. That they hadn't left the townhouse since their arrival eight weeks ago with a baby on each chest hadn't been cause for concern. If she didn't have the time or energy to pull back a curtain, she was certainly in no condition to promenade in St. James Square or waltz the night away at Almack's.

But perhaps it wouldn't even have been an option.

"Would you like to take a stroll with me in the park?" she asked as casually as she could, watching her husband to gauge his interest in ever going back outside.

"We can't." His answer was swift and firm. "We have children."

She nodded and pressed her lips together. "How about we wait until they leave for Eton? Should you fancy a stroll then?"

His blue eyes flashed at her in irritation... but she had not missed the twitch of his fingers or his lack of reply. Her throat tightened.

No. He would not like to venture from these walls. Not today; not twelve years from now. Their home was to be their prison.

Just like her parents' home had been Sarah's prison during the long months of her pregnancy.

"Is it the noise?" she asked. "The weather? Soon it will be summer. Don't you think the boys should enjoy crawling on soft grass in pleasure gardens or splashing with other children at the Peerless Pool on Old Street?"

His jaw tightened. "How should we ferry them there? City streets aren't a safe place for small children. I was nearly run over a dozen times walking from the docks to Mayfair, and I'm a full grown man. There's too many people, far too much noise—"

A knock sounded on the townhouse door.

Edmund leapt from his chair, placing himself in the path between Sarah and the entryway. His muscles visibly tensed at the sound of his footman opening the front door to greet the caller.

Familiar voices spilled into the townhouse.

Edmund whirled around to face Sarah. "It's my parents. Blast. I told them not to come—"

"You told your *parents* not to visit?" she repeated in disbelief.

"They can be... disruptive," he hedged with an embarrassed shrug. "I wanted to give the boys a little time to get used to the world before letting their grandmother loose. I'm surprised she adhered to my edict for this long."

The footman appeared in the doorway. "Master Blackpool, you have—"

"No need to *announce* us. I'm his mother!" Mrs. Blackpool barreled into the sitting room a-flutter. She kissed Edmund's cheek, then Sarah's, and then glanced around the sitting room. "Where are my grandchildren?"

"Sleeping. Good afternoon." Edmund turned to greet his father. "How was the trip up?"

"Long," Mr. Blackpool replied as he handed his coat to the footman. "Have you any cognac?"

"I think so. But I don't know where." Edmund squinted over his shoulder. "Possibly beneath the stairwell."

Sarah blinked. "You keep cognac beneath your stairwell?"

"I stored everything there that used to be in my study when I put together the nursery. The cognac—"

"The *nursery*," breathed Mrs. Blackpool, clasping her hands together. "Let's go at once. I want to see them. I will positively expire if I cannot pinch their little cheeks right this second."

"They're asleep, Mother."

She sniffed in disdain. "You should come live with us. A man's study is no place for infants, Edmund."

"They're not in my study. It's now a nursery."

"Not a proper nursery. This townhouse is a bachelor home. Not at all the thing for a wife and children." She pursed her lips. "I don't know why you're being so stubborn. You know very well that our house in Maidstone has a plethora of empty rooms. Every single one of you could have a bedchamber and a private study by this time tomorrow."

Mr. Blackpool cleared his throat. "There aren't *quite* that many rooms."

"Well, babies don't require studies, do they? It hardly changes my position. By the time they need tutors and governesses, we shall have added on a half dozen additional rooms. Sarah's can be next to mine, Edmund's next to yours, and the babies—"

"Unnecessary, Mother." Edmund linked his fingers with Sarah's. "We appreciate your kind offer, but we won't be moving in with you."

Sarah's shoulders relaxed slightly. The last thing she wanted was to sleep on opposite ends of the house as her husband. He might no longer desire her carnally, but she was quite fond of falling asleep whilst listening to him breathe.

Living with his parents might mean more room, more servants, but if it also meant the end of any hope for a passionate marriage, she would much rather stay in London.

"Edmund, darling," his mother cajoled, her voice a high-pitched coo. "You *must* come live with us. Didn't you enjoy racing down our country hills and playing in the river? Wouldn't you want your twin boys to have the same sort of childhood you and Bartholomew enjoyed?"

He would, Sarah realized, as her husband's stance

stiffened. He was caught between conflicting desires: what was best for his sons and what was best for his sanity. Living in Maidstone would be like having their own private pleasure gardens.

It would also be a living hell.

Mrs. Blackpool meant well—she loved her children far more than what was fashionable, and worried about them ceaselessly—but less than half an hour of her presence had visibly set Edmund's frayed nerves even more on edge. If they shared a roof, Mrs. Blackpool would have opinions on everything, and never cease sharing them. The woman was flighty and dramatic, and kindhearted to the point of obliviousness. She would force their small family to spend every waking moment in the bosom of her love.

"How long can you stay?" Edmund asked his parents. "Can you spend the afternoon with us?"

"I shall stay until you see reason and come back home," his mother returned promptly.

"Then you won't mind sleeping on sofas. 'Tis the only option. If this townhouse had guest quarters, I wouldn't have had to store my study beneath the stairs."

Mrs. Blackpool's cheeks reddened. "I suppose we could stay with Bartholomew. His townhouse is larger, and an inn is wholly out of the question."

Sarah's lips twitched at Mrs. Blackpool's obvious revulsion. Some aristocrats equated inns with sleeping in the rookeries. Sarah imagined Mrs. Blackpool simply refused to let her children out of sight. And definitely not her grandchildren.

Edmund motioned his parents toward the chairs. "Sit. Please. Let me ring for more tea."

"I don't want tea," said Mrs. Blackpool petulantly. "I want to see my grandchildren."

"Mother, for the final time. They are asleep. Try

to understand."

Her cheeks flushed. "I don't need to *speak* with them. I just want to look at them!"

Edmund sighed. "If I had the slightest faith that you could do so quietly…"

"I would never wake a baby!" Mrs. Blackpool shrilled.

Twin wails sounded from upstairs.

"Awake now," said Mr. Blackpool. "Might as well let her see them."

A muscle twitched at Edmund's temple, but he led his parents toward the staircase.

Mrs. Blackpool scurried right behind him, nearly tripping over herself in her eagerness.

"Be thankful all she did was raise her voice," Mr. Blackpool told Sarah conspiratorially. "During the ride to London, I had to talk her out of scaling up the townhouse walls, should the door go unanswered."

She had to hide her smile at the image of flamboyant Mrs. Blackpool climbing row houses like a circus monkey. "We are fortunate indeed that such measures did not prove necessary."

"How are you feeling? I seem to recall after the birth of my sons, my wife took weeks to recover." He frowned. "Edmund says you don't have anyone to help you?"

"Not the case at all," she assured him. "I have Edmund, who is more than simply help. There is nothing he would not do to ensure my comfort, or the safety and well-being of our children. Because of him, I am more than a mother." Her voice cracked on the truth of the words. "Because of him, we are a family."

"Marvelous." He gave her shoulder a brusque pat. "That's all my wife is trying to ascertain."

Sarah nodded, but her mind was focused on Edmund. He wouldn't *be* a good father. He *was* a good father. A wonderful husband.

Was she a wonderful wife? Did she put his comfort and well-being before her own?

Swallowing, she considered the meaning behind Mr. Blackpool's words. For Edmund to have mentioned their lack of nanny or wet nurse meant that their absence bothered him. Sarah had thought such help a spendthrift measure, but perhaps curbing the expense had meant curbing her husband's ability to feel like he was providing for his family to the best of his ability.

Edmund already felt uncomfortable about the limitations of his townhouse. Cognac under the stairs, no guest quarters for his parents... Sarah's heart sank in realization. 'Twasn't just the interior of the small townhouse that bothered Edmund. He hated everything. The busy street, the bustling neighbors, the noisy carriages. He'd nearly jumped out of his skin just from a knock upon the door.

There could only be one reason why he would stay in a location that affected him so viscerally.

He would do it for her.

She was the one who had always talked about London life. The little girl who had longed for fine dresses, and rich food, and waltzes beneath a thousand lit candles.

But she was an adult now. Life was more than gowns and dancing. It meant opening one's heart to those who mattered most.

Up ahead, Edmund was pushing open the door to the nursery and dashing inside to comfort the wailing twins. Upon sight of him, their cries vanished, to be replaced by happy coos.

Sarah held back a smile. Edmund had much the same effect on her.

"They are just *darling*," came Mrs. Blackpool's shrill of delight as Sarah and Mr. Blackpool entered the nursery. "They look exactly like you and Bartholomew did at that age. Now tell me, which one is which?"

"This is Noah," said Edmund as he cuddled the child to his chest.

"And this one is Timothy," Sarah finished as she picked up their other son.

Mrs. Blackpool looked from one to the other several times before throwing up her hands in amused defeat. "Oh, I can't imagine why I bothered to ask. Identical is identical, and I haven't the eye to discern them." She tilted her head at Edmund. "I'm still not completely certain you aren't Bartholomew."

"Mother." With a sardonic expression, Edmund wiggled his right foot. "How can you doubt I'm Edmund?"

"Oh, you're Edmund *now*, that much is certain. But when you were a baby, and even when you were two or three…"

He paled.

"It's quite possible that you were always Edmund," Mr. Blackpool said quickly, upon seeing his son's appalled expression. "I'm almost certain of it."

"May I hold Timothy?" Mrs. Blackpool asked, lifting her outstretched hands toward Edmund.

"*Noah*," Edmund corrected stiffly.

"Noah," Mrs. Blackpool agreed as she brought the infant to her chest and pressed a cheek to his tiny whorl of hair. "They are such darlings. Oh, I wish you would reconsider living in our house. Can't you just picture the twins romping in the garden like you and your brother used to?"

Sarah slid a glance at Edmund. He made no reply.

He didn't have to.

CHAPTER 16

*I*n the middle of the night, Sarah awoke to discover her husband's arm curled protectively around her even in their sleep.

Her heart warmed. Perhaps her life with Edmund wasn't what she'd imagined it would be a year ago, but there was scarcely cause for complaint. Her newborn sons filled her with more love than she'd ever dreamed possible and Edmund was the perfect father, the perfect husband... save for one thing.

He never touched her.

Except that wasn't completely true. There were the little moments. The brush of his thumb against her cheek, his fingers entwining with hers when they rocked their sons side by side, the soft press of his lips to her hair when he thought she was asleep.

And now, this. His arms was tucked about her ribs, just beneath her breasts. Any movement she made would cause the weight of her breasts to drag sensuously across the hard muscle of his arm.

Just thinking about it made her breath quicken.

It had been almost a year since the first—and last—time they'd ever made love. That night in Bruges had been terrifying and magical. For years, she had known Edmund was the one for her. That night had been her opportunity to give herself to him.

Every time she thought back to the feel of hot kisses on her bare skin, she craved to experience it again. To have the sight of his powerful body surging above hers, the scent of sweat and desire intoxicating the air…

Her nipples tightened and pushed up into her thin linen nightrail. If she were alone with her memories, she might slide her hand down between her legs and dip her fingers where her husband's shaft had once filled her.

But she wasn't alone. She had Edmund.

She turned slowly, carefully. Just enough to let her knuckles brush against the front of his nightshirt. His skin was hot through the thin linen. His staff, erect.

Heat flushed her neck and cheeks. She jerked her hand back to her chest, next to her rapidly beating heart. Just because his member was erect did not mean he was dreaming about employing it with her. In Bruges, he had told her that a man's body often became aroused while he was asleep.

He had also told her to take full advantage of it.

Before she could lose her nerve, she turned toward him and touched her hand to his chest. Their thighs now touched, their faces mere inches apart.

His eyes flew open and he tightened his hold about her waist, pulling her even closer.

She gasped, but did not pull away. Instead, she clutched his nightshirt in her fist so that if he let her go, she would pull him down with her.

"Can't sleep?" he murmured, the corners of his eyes crinkling.

She blushed, but held his gaze. "Don't wish to sleep."

"Mmm. I can help with that." A slow, wicked smile

curved his lips. His fingertips began to trace lazy patterns up her spine. "Do you have anything particular in mind?"

"*Everything.*"

She sucked in a breath as he slid his fingers into her hair and brought her parted lips to his.

His mouth was warm and firm. Everything she'd longed for and couldn't have. Until now. As much as his kisses claimed her, she claimed him, too. He wasn't just Edmund. He was *hers*. Her husband. Her soul mate. Her dream come true.

She ran her fingers up the hard planes of his chest to the wide breadth of his shoulder. His body was leaner than it had once been. Stronger. Harder. The feel of his corded muscles beneath her palms was almost like making love to a different person.

If he had been a boy then, he was a man now. There was no hesitation in the passion of his kiss, the demands of his tongue. There was no doubt in the possessiveness of the strong hand cradling her head, her hair entwined with his fingers. She could not break the kiss if she wanted to.

Not that she wished to. She wanted more than mere kisses inflaming her blood. She wanted his big body naked over hers. She wanted to hear him pant with exertion, to feel the sweat on his hot skin as he drove his staff between her legs. She wanted to feel young, and beautiful, and sensuous.

She wanted to be *craved*.

Her body trembled as his hungry kisses lowered to the lobe of her ear, her bare throat. She wanted more. She wanted to feel him everywhere. Already the familiar ache between her legs had her yearning for him to fill her with his shaft.

She grasped his upper arm. He trapped her hand in his and pushed her wrists back against the pillow.

Her heart thundered as his mouth covered the pulse point at the base of her throat and then continued downward toward the loose bodice of her nightrail.

Instead of releasing her wrists in order to tug the neckline of her nightrail below her breasts, he lowered his open mouth to one of her straining nipples and laved it through the thin fabric. Her back arched at the delicious rasp of soft linen, the wet heat of his mouth.

When he freed her wrists to slide the hem of her nightrail from her calves to her hips, her blood soared with anticipation. At last, he would bury his shaft within her. At last, he would once again be hers. Heart racing in excitement, she widened her legs to give him easier access.

Instead of instantly driving within her, he spread her legs with his strong hands and buried his face between them.

The wicked mouth that had just been on her breast now covered her most private of places. From the first lick of his skilled tongue, pressure began to build within her, demanding release. Each lick, each suckle, had her muscles tensing with desire.

Eyes shut tight to better experience the onslaught of sensation, she reached down to grasp a handful of his tousled hair. Not to stop him, not to pull him up, but to ensure he stayed right where he was, because the pressure was growing growing growing and her legs were already beginning to quiver with anticipation.

As his tongue continued its intoxicating pattern, he slipped two of his fingers into her tight sheath, thrusting with every lick.

She gasped as delirious waves of pleasure rocked through her, clenching her muscles and her toes and leaving her insensate.

THE BRIGADIER'S RUNAWAY BRIDE

When at last he lifted his mouth from her body, she raised her head to bid him do the same with his rod—and saw that the entire front of her bodice was soaking wet. Mortification flushed her cheeks. Had she been spurting *breastmilk* while her husband pleasured her?

With his gaze still focused between her legs, Edmund started to push her nightrail higher.

She scrambled backward toward the headboard, covering her leaking breasts with one arm as she shoved down the hem of her nightrail with the other. Embarrassment paralyzed her. She couldn't possibly make love to him like *this*.

What had she been thinking? Worse yet would have been the shame if he had divested her of her nightrail. In the past seven weeks, she'd managed to lose most of her excess weight… but her stomach was now flabby, and crisscrossed with white stretch lines. What man would be attracted to that?

Brow furrowed, he pulled himself into a sitting position. "Is something the matter?"

She gulped. What wasn't the matter? She might as well admit it. Theirs was a romance built on physical desire, and her new body was far from desirable. Even to her. She couldn't bear to disappoint her husband. Not when she wanted his desire so much.

He tilted his head, his expression confused. "Sarah?"

A baby's shrill cry sounded from the nursery.

"I have to tend to the children." She scrambled from the bed with alacrity, pausing only to snatch a clean robe from the back of a chair before she flew out the door.

The white scars striping her belly would never go away, but she couldn't make love to him like this. A smart woman would wait until the moment was right. Until her body was as close to what it had once been as possible. A smart woman would dress in a provocative gown. Set the scene for a romantic evening. A smart woman would not take the risk of having him turn from her in repulsion. Perhaps extinguish the fire altogether so he could not see what she had become.

Her hands shook as she clutched the robe to her swollen breasts. She wanted him so much and loved him so deeply. If she bared her soul and he no longer wanted her, her heart would break forever.

CHAPTER 17

*E*dmund shoved boxes out from under the stairwell until he finally unearthed his missing bottle of cognac.

He slumped against one of the dusty walls, propped his booted feet atop the closest crate, and uncorked the last few inches of golden liquid. The bottle predated his commission into the army, but a sniff of its contents indicated the contents were just as sweet and fragrant as ever.

With a sigh, he recorked the bottle and put it back into the box.

To him, spirits were a celebration. A toast to a new life or a tribute to a job well done. He had a new life, all right, but he didn't deserve commendation. He deserved castigation. He had pushed Sarah before she was ready.

The back of his head thunked against the stairwell. Damn it all. He had sworn to himself he would give her time to adjust to her new home, her new children, her new husband, everything. He had *seen* what she'd had to suffer to give birth and had no doubt it would take time to recover. She was as beautiful today as the day they'd met, but that didn't mean she wasn't still healing. Even if she had reached for him first.

A distant knock rapped against the front door and Edmund's body tensed. He supposed that was an improvement. Until recently, his normal reaction to startling noises had become diving for cover lest he be shot in the chest.

His footman materialized outside the open stairwell door.

"Don't tell me." Edmund pushed to his feet and ducked out of the low cubby. "My parents are back."

The footman smiled. "Major Bartholomew Blackpool to see you, sir."

Edmund's twin came into view wearing champagne-shined Hessians, spotless buckskin breeches, an exquisitely carved walking stick, a sapphire blue tailcoat with sparkling gold buttons, a coal black top hat, and an explosion of starched white linen protruding from his neck.

Bartholomew grinned and affected a formal bow. "Brother."

Edmund wiped stairwell dust from his hands to his wrinkled trousers. "Please tell me you've come because you've missed me, and not because Mother has been overstaying her welcome in London and you want me to do something about it."

Bartholomew's eyes widened. "Did she truly leave Maidstone? I had no idea."

Edmund squinted at him. "They were here not a fortnight ago, and I could swear she intended to pay a long visit to you."

"Well, she might have intended such, but Daphne and I were in South Tyneside with the miners, then over to Littleport to see about the wheat farmers, and then of course there's the situation brewing in Manchester..." Bartholomew lifted a shoulder.

"Truth be told, we just got back to London this afternoon."

Edmund motioned for his brother to follow him to the sitting room. "And your first act upon returning to Town was to visit me? I'm flattered, brother, but should you not be relaxing at home?"

Bartholomew burst out laughing. "Have you met my wife? Daphne has no idea what relaxing means. 'Twas all I could do to talk her out of inspecting every weaving loom in Lancashire. Now that we're home, she's decided we ought to go to Vauxhall to see the orchestra and the fireworks. Any chance you two would like to join us?"

Edmund's stomach clenched. "None. I doubt Sarah could bear to be more than a few feet from the twins."

Bartholomew flopped into one of the wingback chairs. "I presumed as much."

Edmund, on the other hand, was having a moment of doubt. *He* couldn't think of anything less relaxing than standing amongst a teeming crush of people while loud explosions sounded overhead.

Sarah, on the other hand, might find the pleasure gardens a welcome distraction.

She hadn't been more than a few feet from the twins since the moment of their birth. Constant proximity had been as much Edmund's design as any particular requirement of the babies'. They needed to be fed every few hours, but that didn't mean someone else couldn't keep a watchful eye on them while she and Edmund took a turn about the park or did a bit of shopping.

She'd as much as begged him for just such a brief respite and he had refused out of hand. Repeatedly. The streets were dangerous, unpredictable… but to Sarah, they were home.

Bartholomew leaned forward, frowning. "Is something amiss, brother?"

Edmund shook his head. Nothing at all was amiss, other than his realization that his wife's rejection of further advances might not have had anything to do with her physical recovery. After all, she was the one who had initiated the lovemaking. She would not have done so if her body were not ready.

Thus the problem didn't lie with her, but with him. Could he blame her? He wasn't the same man as when he'd first left, or even the same man who'd thought nothing of meeting a lover in Bruges. He was a man who wouldn't let his wife or children leave their minuscule townhouse. Perhaps Sarah had simply wished to make love to a husband, not a gaoler.

The staircase creaked.

Edmund glanced up to see his wife descending the stairs. His jaw tightened. She hadn't spoken to him since the previous night. She'd waited until he was asleep before returning to the bedchamber, then feigned sleep of her own until he'd quit the room in the morning.

He hoped this wouldn't become their new routine. He loved her too much to live like that. But if she was waiting for him to rent a phaeton to go racing on Rotten Row... well, she'd be waiting a long time.

"Bartholomew!" Sarah's warm voice was filled with genuine pleasure. "What a lovely surprise. I'll ring for tea."

Edmund's eyes met Bartholomew's over the empty table and they both hid smiles. Edmund supposed he couldn't feel slighted that Sarah hadn't bothered to ask if he'd already rung for tea... because,

THE BRIGADIER'S RUNAWAY BRIDE

of course, he hadn't. He'd been thinking of her, not his brother.

"What are you doing in London?" Sarah asked Bartholomew after joining Edmund on the sofa. "I thought Daphne didn't expect to be back home until late June."

She hadn't? Edmund cast his wife an inquiring glance. Her gaze was fixed on Bartholomew. Edmund frowned and tried not to feel left out. If Sarah wished to correspond with Daphne, she had every right to do so. They had been acquainted for years, and even if they hadn't, writing letters was likely the sole source of non-baby entertainment to be found inside the townhouse.

"Yes, well, that was the idea, but..." Bartholomew took a deep breath. "Daphne is going to be a mother."

Sarah gasped and clapped her hands together. "That's splendid!"

Edmund grinned. "Congratulations, brother."

"I'm scared out of my skull." Bartholomew dropped his head into his hands. "That's why I'm here."

Edmund arched a brow. "You're worried it'll be twins?"

"I'm worried they'll be *girls*," Bartholomew confessed in terror. "How the devil will I ever keep up with three Daphnes?"

Sarah laughed. "Well, the first thing to know—"

"—is that you're going to do everything wrong," Edmund finished wryly. "But it will end up just fine."

The blood drained from Bartholomew's face. "Wrong? Like what? Perhaps I can avoid the same mistakes."

"Little things. The first time I burped the baby, I had just donned fresh clothes." Sarah smiled at the memory. "He spit up all over me and I didn't have another chance to bathe for an hour."

Bartholomew recoiled in horror. "He spit up on your *clothes?*"

Sarah made a face. "After that, I learned to keep clean rags on my shoulders."

"Their drool gets everywhere," Edmund said with a shake of his head. "They like to gnaw my fingers, my cravat…"

"My hair, my cheek… One time, even my nose." Sarah laughed.

Bartholomew looked appalled. "I will let someone else burp them. Thank you for the sound advice."

"And then there's the baths," Edmund said. "If I were you, I wouldn't wear white to—"

"Hire a nanny." Sarah made eyes at her husband to leave his dandy brother in peace. Bartholomew would not be able to handle the bath stories. "The biggest difference in our lives was the constant exhaustion. The first few weeks are definitely the most difficult."

"I don't think we slept," Edmund agreed.

"I *know* we didn't. Remember the time the twins were fussing to be fed, and you accidentally brought me the same one twice?"

"Or the time you went to put Noah in his cradle and got confused because he was already in there sleeping?"

"It was Timothy!" She gasped with laughter at the memory and touched her head briefly to Edmund's shoulder. "How about the time you were so wet with bathwater that you took off your ruined shirt and Noah tried to suckle your nipple?"

"Or the time you lifted Timothy from the bath and suffered an attack of hysteria because you thought his bollocks were missing?"

"They vanished!" she protested, her face flaming red. "How was *I* to know cold water has such an effect on young boys?"

"Tea?" said the footman as he placed the tray on the table with an impressively expressionless face.

"Have you anything stronger?" Bartholomew asked weakly.

Edmund smiled. "Old cognac."

"Under the stairwell," Sarah clarified.

Bartholomew glanced at the open stairwell then back at Edmund's dusty breeches. "Tea will do."

Edmund cocked his head. "I thought you gave up spirits."

"I thought this was a fine time to start anew." Bartholomew accepted a freshly poured cup from Sarah. "How have you managed it?"

She cast Edmund a tentative smile. "Together, my husband and I can do anything."

He reached for her hand before responding to his brother. "At first, I felt like a total failure. I was constantly trying to keep up, trying to guess what the twins needed, trying to recall what I'd already done. I couldn't keep track of what day it was, much less anything else. But then we got into a routine and things went smoother. The twins were calmer, happier. Even started sleeping longer."

"The first time they slept through the night, I panicked," Sarah admitted. "I was convinced if they weren't crying, it was because they'd stopped breathing, or that something was wrong. Edmund had to practically shake me out of my hysteria to get me to see they were breathing just fine and had fallen asleep." She held his hand to her face. "By then, I'd woken them up and they *did* start crying."

"They quieted down right away." He stroked her cheek with his thumb, then turned to his brother.

"The point is, people have been having babies for thousands of years. There will be frightening moments and exhausting moments, but more than anything—"

"—there will just be love," Sarah finished. "More than your heart can handle. There are no words to describe the awe of holding your newborn infant in your arms."

"...or their tiny fist closing about your finger..."

"...cradling them in your arms..." Her eyes went dreamy.

"...the way their eyes light up when they first recognize you..."

"...the smell of their skin..."

"...how they both have a single tuft of curly hair..." He lifted a piece of his own to portray the tuftiness of it.

Sarah waved him away. "They're perfect angels. I adore their cunning little baby gowns..."

"I adore the way they snore like lumbermen..."

"Noah does not snore!" she huffed.

Edmund arched a brow. "What's he doing, then? Speaking 'pig' to us?"

She cuffed him on the shoulder before turning to Bartholomew. "You'll see. It's the little things that make everything so worth it. Just the way they snuggle into my chest as if there's nowhere else they'd rather be..."

"There's nowhere else *I'd* rather be," Edmund stage-whispered to his brother.

A cry sounded from upstairs.

Sarah squeezed Edmund's hand before letting go to rise to her feet. "If you'll excuse me, gentlemen."

They both leapt to their feet until she'd disappeared up the stairs.

"You're happy, then? With everything?" asked

Bartholomew once they'd retaken their chairs. "Not only did it take longer than hoped to reunite with Sarah, your return home wasn't as smooth as one might've liked."

"Happier than I'd ever imagined," Edmund assured his brother. He was not surprised to find it was true. There were things he hoped might improve, but there was nothing he would wish away. "Neither my long trek home nor the circumstances of my reunion with Sarah were any fault of yours, brother."

Bartholomew flinched. "I cannot help but feel ashamed for my cursed silence. I am sorry I did not tell you immediately about what had really happened at Waterloo."

Edmund shook his head. "Don't be absurd. Were you meant to shout it out in front of everyone? I had already crashed the wedding, so there was no hope of making a bigger commotion than that."

Bartholomew swallowed. "Ravenwood—"

"—was being a true friend. I might not have seen it at the time, but I see it now." Edmund's smile was wry. "All of you were willing to sacrifice for the sake of my unborn children. How could I condemn any of you for that?"

His brother seemed unconvinced. "Oliver felt wretched about being forced to choose one of us to save."

"I forgive Oliver. His choices were limited."

"*I* felt wretched for being the one that he'd saved." Anguish filled Bartholomew's face.

Edmund softened his voice. "I forgive *you*, brother. You didn't have a choice. Besides, had the decision been left to me... I would have made the same choice."

"As would I," Bartholomew said fiercely, his eyes glistening. "Given half the chance."

"You would save yourself?" Edmund teased.

"I would have to, for Mother England." Bartholomew peered down his nose at Edmund's dusty attire. "With that cravat, you embarrass the entire country."

Edmund's throat tightened. He had missed his twin dreadfully. The teasing. The camaraderie. The sense of belonging. Of being half of a whole.

"I love you too, brother," he said gruffly, then popped a biscuit into his mouth before he could be forced to say it again.

CHAPTER 18

When the supper gong sounded, Sarah stepped out of the nursery just in time to collide with her husband. He caught her in his arms and did not immediately release her.

A familiar warmth spread through her at the feel of her breasts pressing up against the hard strength of his body. Not just a familiar warmth. A familiar *want*. An endless aching need that made it impossible to let him go.

"May I escort you to the table?" he asked, his words a soft whisper caressing the shell of her ear.

She nodded jerkily. She had no voice to do anything else. Her pulse pounded. Had she been able to respond, she would not have invited him to the supper table, but to their bedchamber. To the bed they should have been sharing all along.

He proffered his arm.

She slipped her fingers about his elbow and reveled in the strength of his muscles beneath her palm. She missed his touch. In keeping him from seeing her unsightly new body, she had been keeping herself from enjoying his.

The brief passion they had shared the other night

had not extinguished her ardor, but inflamed it. Now she could not look at him without remembering his mouth, his fingers, his tongue.

When they reached the bottom of the stairs, he paused but did not let her go. She held her breath as his hot gaze met hers. He, too, was not thinking about food. Their interlude had awakened his passions as well as his own. She had but to say the word, and he would carry her right back up these stairs.

Her mouth dried. She was too frightened to say yes. Too aroused to say no. He was right here. He was hers. This was their chance at a better future. Her body yearned for his touch. Needed to feel him, to have him.

She was tired of waiting. Of letting fear limit her marriage. She wanted all of him.

Tonight.

A loud crash sounded just outside the front window.

Edmund tackled her to the carpet before the first screams even rent the air. He lay across her in a protective shell, his back toward the danger, his eyes glassy and unseeing as the clatter continued.

Her heart was racing, but not nearly as loud or as fast as her husband's. The color had drained from his face in seconds, leaving his skin pasty white and slick with sweat.

He didn't move. Not a twitch of a muscle, nor even a rise and fall to his chest. Were it not for his hot, clammy flesh, he could as easily be a statue. Or a cadaver.

She reached up to touch his face. "Edmund?"

"It's a carriage accident." His voice was empty.

"Yes. Outside."

His body began to shake. "I told you it was dangerous. Someone might have died. Perhaps several people did. It sounded…"

"Darling, I'm right here. It wasn't me or the twins." She caressed his cheek. "We're safe. Your family is safe."

"It *could* be you. Not today. Tomorrow." His voice cracked. "I won't *let* it be you. I won't let… I can't…"

She pulled him into her arms and stroked his hair. "I know you won't. I trust you. You'll keep us safe."

His body began to shiver.

She held him in her arms until the squeals of horses and metal faded away and the shouts in the street finally quieted. She held him until her arms trembled from maintaining the same position for minutes, hours. She held him until he could feel her love, feel the beating of her heart, feel his wife alive and safe beneath him.

He rolled onto his back and pulled her into his arms. Now that the noise was gone, he could breathe heavily. She pressed her ear to his chest. His heart thundered alarmingly. The linen of his shirt was damp with sweat.

"I'm sorry." The vibrations of his voice rumbled against her cheek. "You must think me as prone to hysteria as my mother."

She reached up to thread her fingers in his hair. "Nothing of the sort. You are right. It *was* a carriage accident."

"A bad one."

"Yes," she agreed.

"The screams…" He shuddered as if he'd caught a sudden chill. "The horses…"

Her throat tightened. "It reminded you of Waterloo?"

His muscles tensed. "It didn't remind me. It took me there. As if no time had passed at all."

They lay for a long time in silence.

"I won't ask if it was awful," she said in a soft voice, "because I know it was. Nor will I ask for details you're not ready to share. Just know that I am here—*right* here—if ever you need me."

"I don't want to talk about the war," he said after a moment. "Ever."

She nodded against his heart. "That's fine."

He hesitated. "But I will tell you what happened after."

She mentally prepared herself for the worst. "After being shot?"

"After waking up." He took a deep breath and his heartbeat settled slightly. "A week had passed. I think. It was impossible to judge time."

"You had been taken to a hospital?"

"A Flemish convent. Deep in the countryside. They had row after row of soldiers…"

"How did you get there?"

"I never knew. I couldn't ask. I didn't speak Dutch then."

She blinked. "Do you speak Dutch now?"

"I had to learn in order to survive."

Her mouth fell open in outrage. "They treated you badly at the convent?"

He shook his head. "Anything but. The nuns were miracle workers. Most of the soldiers died, but 'twasn't their fault. To wind up in one of their cots meant you had been given up for dead."

She snuggled into him and held on tight.

"All I had was what I was wearing. That's all any of us had. Bloodstained uniforms with bullet holes or pieces missing." His words came choppier now. "As soon as it was clear I might survive, they gave me a clean set of clothes. Likely cobbled together from scraps of usable cloth taken from the uniforms of dead men."

Sarah shivered.

"A great many of us had been trampled by fleeing men and fleeing horses." He gazed into the distance. "It took months to recover, to learn to walk again, to pick up a heavy object."

"Were there many heavy objects?"

"*Many.*" His lips twisted. "I had no money, no people, no way to communicate. Once I left the convent, my only choice was to take any odd job I could find, for any pay I could scrabble. Sometimes it was a scrap of food, a hayloft for a bed. Other times, it wasn't even a sou. I couldn't argue, because I didn't speak the language."

"But you learned," she said quietly.

He nodded. "I learned."

She held him tight.

"I learned to muck out stalls," he continued presently, his voice flat. "To clear quarries. To build stone fences. I learned about hunger. I learned botflies from horses could lay their worms in humans. I learned how to walk for miles and miles, with or without shoes."

"You were heading to the coast?"

"First, to Waterloo. I didn't realize how much time had passed. At first, I didn't know the war was over. If the troops were still there... If my brother was still alive..."

She lifted her head. "Who was left at Waterloo when you arrived?"

"No one." His voice was flat, his eyes haunted. "By the time I got there, even the fallen's teeth had been squirreled away for making sets of false teeth. There was nothing left for me. Nothing and no one."

She burrowed into him. "Did you try to catch the troops?"

"I didn't care about the troops. I cared about Bartholomew. Oliver. Xavier. What if I was the sole survivor? What if I'd walked a hundred miles until the clothes rotted off my back, and there was nobody left to find?"

Her heart pounded. She couldn't imagine the terror of such a moment.

"But there was always you," he said quietly.

She stared up at him. "Me?"

"You were safe in England. Safe and alive. All I had to do…" He swallowed. "…was return to you."

"And you did," she said softly.

"You were the one thought that kept me moving forward. The dream that kept me sane." He lifted his hand to his waistcoat pocket, then pressed a scrap of silk into her palm.

Her mouth curved in wonder. "The stocking ribbon you stole in Bruges! But how—"

"I stayed alive for you, Sarah." His eyes were intense, magnetic, as he lowered his lips to hers. "I knew finding you would mean I'd come home."

CHAPTER 19

After supper, as Sarah went upstairs to nurse her children, her heart was heavy. Her husband had been through something unimaginable... and, quite possibly, insurmountable in their current environment.

The carriage accident had indeed caused fatalities. The footman had stepped outside to get the news. It was dreadful.

A chimney boy had darted in front of the horses to retrieve his master's top hat, which had been taken by the wind. The horses had startled, and reared. The child had been kicked to the ground. The driver had tried desperately to control his horses. The hackney coach behind him—unaware of what was happening—tried to pass the first carriage, but the panicked horses incited his own. When the two carriages collided, the first carriage became imbalanced and careened to its side.

The driver and passengers were bruised, but would survive with little harm.

The chimney boy trapped beneath the horses and fallen carriage would not.

Startled horses or broken axles occurred with

regularity, but rarely was the outcome fatal. Sarah doubted that fact would bring much solace to her husband. If he had been apprehensive before about the safety of his children on the street, he certainly wouldn't allow the twins out of the townhouse now.

Not after a child had been killed right outside his door.

Sarah shivered as she gazed down at the suckling infant in her arms. She was not a fearful person, but the terrifying proceedings had unsettled her as much as it had her husband.

Well, no. They hadn't reacted *exactly* the same.

Edmund, she had to admit, was not meant to live in the city. Perhaps neither were she and the twins. As suffocating as it would be to go from privacy to living with his mother, the countryside would no doubt be a much better place for Edmund to raise his sons. Safer. Happier. More peaceful.

She would tell him tonight. The day he deemed the children old enough to travel, off to Kent they would go. She would not put him through this torture a moment longer.

Maidstone would be better for all of them. They would finally be able to go out-of-doors. To enjoy life.

As a family.

She tucked the last infant into his cradle after his feeding and touched a hand to her unsightly stomach. It didn't matter. The scars, the loose skin—none of it mattered. What mattered was her family.

Sarah was a good mother. Of that, she had no doubt. There was nothing she wouldn't do for her children.

She was also a good wife. Or at least, she tried to be. She loved Edmund more than her heart could hold. She hadn't wanted to disappoint him with what her body had become... but her body was *her*. Just because she couldn't undo the effects of pregnancy and childbirth, did that mean she was to withhold the physical love they both needed for the rest of their lives?

He deserved love. *She* deserved love. The one thing they should always be able to count on was each other.

Tonight, she would prove it.

She shook the wrinkles from her day dress as best she could and pushed fallen tendrils of hair back into the twist behind her head. Her babies had just been fed, so she would not need to fear another embarrassing leak. She only had to fear her husband's rejection.

Her fingers trembled. If he were repulsed by her body... if he could no longer make love to her, her heart would break. But she would no longer prevent him from trying. She forced her spine straight and adjusted her bodice. Not tonight. Right now.

She would seduce her husband.

She strode out the nursery door. Edmund, she discovered, was at the fireplace in their bedchamber stoking a few orange embers into a fire. His jacket lay across the back of one of the small sitting chairs, leaving his shirtsleeves to billow about his arm muscles as he worked.

Sarah paused in the doorway to watch. She loved the singleminded concentration he focused on everything he did. She loved the strength in his body. Watching his muscles move. She loved how the crackling fire cast a warm glow over his hands and profile, highlighting his strong chin, his firm lips, his dark brow.

She loved Edmund.

When he replaced the poker in its stand and

turned to face her, she realized he was not surprised at her presence. He'd known she was watching him. And had given her the space to do as she willed.

His eyes met hers. Blue. Arresting.

"Have you come to mother me because of my outburst?"

She shook her head. "I've come to seduce you."

His pupils dilated as his gaze heated.

She smiled. He hadn't been surprised at her presence, but he'd been very surprised at the reason.

He held up a palm. "By all means."

Heart pounding in sudden nervousness, she turned and headed for the bed.

He did not follow her.

She bit her lip. "Aren't you joining me in bed?"

"Aren't you going to seduce me?" he countered softly.

Her eyes widened.

He was right. Had their roles been reversed, the seduction would have to begin long before they tumbled into bed. She cocked her head and gazed at him for a moment.

What would seduce her husband? Should she untie her garter ribbons and roll down her stockings one inch at a time? Or should she grab him by the hand, boldly, beguilingly, and tug him beside her underneath the covers?

None of those things, she decided. She was no longer a coquette, nor would she allow herself to keep hiding her body. This was a new kind of seduction. Her husband stood before the fireplace. Therefore, she would go to him.

She approached the fireplace without attempting to mask her nervous hesitance with false confidence. She was Sarah. For better or for worse. And she would seduce him without pretending to be anything other than who she was.

Stepping out of her slippers and onto the thick carpet made her feel bolder. The soft texture against the silk of her stockings meant she had *begun*. There was no going back. There was only Edmund.

She took his fingers in hers. "Good evening, husband."

"Good evening, wife." His eyes glittered in the firelight.

She gestured toward one of the chairs. "Please, have a seat. Allow me to remove your boots."

He chose the closest one and sat. He dwarfed the slender chair. It was armless and expertly carved and had barely been used in the two months they'd been living here. They'd been too busy with the infants to take time for themselves.

Until now.

She sank to her knees before him and placed her hands around the ankle of one of his tall leather Hessians. As she tugged each boot free, she did not look at her hands, but rather kept her eyes on her husband's face.

He was gazing at her with an intensity that made her toes curl.

She set his boots aside and ran her hands up his calves, over his knees, onto his legs, close to his lap. Then she spun around, nestling her back between his knees, and lifted the stray tendrils from the nape of her neck to expose her spine.

"Unbutton me?" The words were spoken as a question, but they both knew it was not. He had been waiting for this moment just as long as she had.

With a growl, he placed his strong fingers against her spine and made short work of unfastening her gown.

She did not retreat. The dress gaped along her back, but there were two more layers beneath. "Now my stays."

For nine months, she hadn't worn them.

There were no stays on earth wide enough to accommodate her pregnant body. For the first month after giving birth, her less rotund form could technically be bound by whalebone and quilted linen, but the excess bits bulging out the top of the stays did more harm than good to her silhouette.

About a fortnight ago, she'd realized most of her body had returned close enough to its original width to employ stays anew. 'Twas ironic. Where once she had cursed the inflexible busk's ability to inhibit movement, she now rejoiced in the ability to cage herself in it at all. Stays might not be the most comfortable of women's underclothing, but they made her feel feminine and pretty—something she'd desperately needed.

Feeling her husband's large fingers gently loosen the corded ribbon made every moment of her beauty toilette worth it. She felt like herself again. Like she was someone desirable.

Once her stays were loosened, she placed her palms atop her husband's legs and rose to her feet. Keeping her gaze locked on his, she pushed her day dress off her shoulders and let it slide to the floor.

Edmund swallowed. His hands clamped the tops of his legs as if he were forcing himself not to reach for her.

She unfastened the front of her stays and dropped them onto the other chair. She would not be sitting there. She would be right here, seducing her husband.

Freed from its bindings, her thin white chemise fluttered against her naked body. Cool air and low heat from the nearby fire sent warmth and gooseflesh chasing across her skin.

She was nervous in a way she hadn't been a year ago, in Bruges. The first time they'd made love, her biggest fear was the actual mechanics. How much it might hurt. Whether her ignorance would disappoint him.

She no longer had any fear of the act itself. She'd spent long, aching nights yearning for his touch. Now he was here, in front of her. Waiting to be seduced. She touched her fingertips to his chest.

"I dislike this waistcoat."

He raised his brows. "What's wrong with it?"

"You're still wearing it." She arched a brow.

He shrugged out of his waistcoat in a matter of seconds. "Happy?"

She shook her head. "I seem to also have strong feelings against your shirt. Its presence offends my sensibilities."

He crossed his arms at his waist to pull the offending garment up and over his head, but she stopped him.

She lifted the edge of her chemise just high enough to allow her to straddle his thighs. Perched atop him, her breasts were now at the same height as his parted lips.

Slowly, she tugged the shirt free from his waistband. Little by little, she eased it up over the muscled planes of his abdomen, up over corded scars crisscrossing his chest, up over his head and off into the shadows.

She lowered her head and brushed her lips against his. "Are you going to kiss me?"

"Are you?" he growled.

She smiled. "Absolutely."

Her heart pounded as she suckled his lower lip into her mouth, kissing, licking, tasting. Wanting.

At last he wrapped her in his arms, sinking his fingers into her hair and holding her to him as his mouth devoured hers with kisses.

The familiar sensual ache began to pool between her legs. This time, she wasn't lying frightened in the shadows, afraid to let him touch her. This time, she was astride his strong thighs. Trapping him between her breasts and the chair.

Her breath quickened. She felt powerful. Beautiful. *Desired*.

She tore her mouth from his, panting, and brought her lips to his ear. "Make love to me."

"Make me." He pressed a trail of hot kisses down the curve of her throat. He trapped the edge of her bodice in his teeth and jerked the thin linen down to expose her breasts.

She gasped as his tongue dragged sensuously over her nipples. Her body was more than ready for him. Every inch of her was trembling with anticipation, begging him to make her his.

Make me, he'd challenged her. Very well. She couldn't wait any longer.

She gathered her chemise up to her waist and reached her hand between their bodies to unbutton the fall of his breeches. His shaft sprang free to rub tantalizingly against the heat of her slick core. Thrilled at her own boldness, she touched her fingers to her sensitive cleft then wrapped her wet fingers around his erect member.

His mouth slackened, his entire body stiffening in pleasure. She rose up on her toes to position his shaft at her opening and then slowly, deliciously, sank back down until he was fully sheathed.

His mouth captured hers, giving, taking. He

gripped her hips as she rode him, letting her guide the rhythm.

She wrapped her arms about his neck. He was her anchor. Her tempest.

He closed his fist about her chemise, raising the hem to lift it over her head.

She froze. Not because she wanted to make it easier for him to remove her chemise—but because her brain had flooded with all the fears of how he would react once he had done so.

His eyes met hers just as he lifted the hem breast height and he paused in concern. "What is it?"

A flush crept across her skin. "I just… want you to think me beautiful."

"You *are* beautiful." He tore the chemise over her head and took her mouth in a searing kiss. "You think I married you for your beauty? Bloody right, I did." His hands cradled her face. "Nothing can ever take it from you. You'll be beautiful to me when you're eighty years old and missing most of your teeth."

She swallowed. "It's already too late. My body…"

"How could I fail to love your body? I love *you*." He rocked his hips so she would feel his shaft buried deep within her. "You're everything. With you, the past melts away. With you, I have a future."

Her back arched as his words washed over her. *He loved her*. She lifted up and sank back down, taking him into her body and her heart. "I thought you would hate my scars. I thought you wouldn't want me."

He lifted her breasts to his face and ran his tongue across the sensitive nipples. "I will always want you. I have my scars, you have yours. Scars aren't ugly, darling. They're visible signs of how strong you are."

"How strong *we* are," she said, her voice breathless

at the twin sensations of his mouth on her breasts as his shaft drove within her.

"I'm yours, Sarah," he said between kisses. "I would cross the world to be with you. To feel your body wrapped around me and know you were mine forever."

The pressure built so strong, she was certain she would shatter against him. "Edmund, please—"

"Thank God." He gripped her hips, his fingers digging into her to ride her faster.

She gasped as her muscles clenched around him, pleasure filling her until she was spent and breathless.

He wrapped his arms around her and she sagged against him in sated wonder. She was in love. *He* was in love. Their future was wide open. She lay her cheek against his shoulder and held him close. They weren't just a family…

They would live happily ever after.

CHAPTER 20

*E*dmund's mother tore from her house with shrieks of joy as he and his wife carefully descended from a hired hack with their children in their arms.

"You bad boy," she scolded delightedly. "You terrible son. Why did you not tell me you might come for a visit? I would have filled the entire house with biscuits for my grandchildren!"

"They don't have teeth yet, Mother."

She waved this away. "Jellies, then. Marmalade. The point is, these adorable little gentlemen should enjoy every moment at their grandmother's house. How am I expected to craft the perfect visit if I don't even know you're coming?"

"Our deepest apologies," said Sarah, her eyes twinkling.

Edmund's mother sniffed. "Yes, well. It's enough to give one vapors. Do keep that in mind next time. And come inside, come inside! Unless you wish to show the twins the river? I could have commissioned boats, had I known you were coming! Of all the ill-mannered… How long can you stay? A month, at least. Perhaps three or four. The Season is over, which means there isn't any reason to return to London until Christmastide at the earliest."

Edmund affected a deep sigh. "We can only stay an hour, I'm afraid."

"An *hour?*" His mother stared at him as if she truly might have a fit of the vapors. Her face blanched. "You can't travel all the way back to London after just one hour when it took you all day to get here!"

"Actually," he said with a slow smile. "It didn't."

"But how…?"

Sarah stepped forward and pointed down the hill in the direction in which they'd come. "We've a cottage not more than a mile from here, on the bank of the river."

Edmund's mother clasped her hands together, eyes shining as tears spilled down her cheeks. "You're the *best* daughter. And the best son. We'll be the happiest family who ever lived."

Edmund smiled at his parents, his children, his wife. "I believe we already are."

EPILOGUE

*E*dmund shook out the twins' favorite blanket, faded from repeated use beneath the sun, and smoothed it atop a patch of sprightly green grass. He held out a hand to Sarah, and they arranged themselves in familiar comfortable positions from which he could stroke her hair whilst keeping a sharp eye on the rambunctious boys playing beneath the tall, leafy trees.

Country life was perfect. He had his wife, his sons, and a beautiful, peaceful environment in which to enjoy them.

His parents lived just close enough to offer the boys frequent stays at their grandparents' house, yet far enough away that Edmund and Sarah had plenty of opportunity for privacy, romance, and frequent family outings like this one.

"Do you miss London?" he asked her.

She glanced up at him, her head in his lap and her eyes round with surprise. "Not in the least. Why, darling? Reminiscing about your fashionable townhouse?"

"Hardly." He stifled a laugh at the thought.

From the moment he'd returned to his townhouse, he couldn't wait to leave it behind. Everything he'd thought he'd wanted—the noise, the bustle, the sights, the smells—had become his worst nightmares. Escaping the city had let him enjoy his family, instead of caging them indoors to protect them.

Not to mention what a boon the influx of income had been for them after he'd sold his high-priced townhouse. Between his savings and the money the Army had owed him, they needn't worry about money. All Edmund had to provide was time and love—two things he possessed in great abundance.

"I was thinking..." He rubbed the pad of his thumb against his wife's cheek.

Her eyes fluttered closed. "Mm? What about?"

"Don't you think our sons ought to have...a sister? The boys shouldn't have all our attention."

Sarah flashed him a mischievous grin and pulled herself up in his lap to press a kiss against his jaw. "Indeed. I myself have one or two things I wouldn't mind turning your attention to..."

"Oh?" He brushed his lips against hers and smiled. Nightfall couldn't come quickly enough. "I am eager to be of service."

She wrapped her arms about his neck. "How did I ever get so lucky?"

"The best day of my life was the day I met you." He kissed the tip of her nose, then raised his eyebrows toward the twins. "The second best was the night we created those rapscallions."

"That was an exceptional night," she agreed. "But the highlight of mine was the day you barged into Ravenwood's estate and stopped that wedding. It was a dream come true. You are a dream come true. I love you more every day."

He smiled wickedly. "And every night?"

She grinned back. "Especially then."

He held her close as the sun slowly began to dip toward the horizon. For a man who had once lost everything, he now had everything he hadn't even dared to hope for. His freedom. His family. His life.

And a love that would last forever.

THE END

～

A desperate Earl of Carlisle sent a swaggering buccaneer to America to fetch his betrothed's mother. How do you suppose that turned out?

Find out in *The Pirate's Tempting Stowaway*!

～

Don't forget your free book!

Sign up at http://ridley.vip for members-only exclusives, including advance notice of pre-orders, as well as contests, giveaways, freebies, and 99¢ deals!

THANK YOU FOR READING

Not a VIP yet? Grab a FREE book!

Sign up at https://ridley.vip for members-only exclusives, including advance notice of pre-orders, as well as contests, giveaways, freebies, and 99¢ deals!

∾

Love talking books with fellow readers?

Join the *Historical Romance Book Club* for prizes, books, and live chats with your favorite romance authors:
Facebook.com/groups/HistRomBookClub

Check out the **Patreon** for bonus content, sneak peeks, advance review copies and more:
Patreon.com/EricaRidleyFans

And don't miss the **official website**:
EricaRidley.com

THE PIRATE'S TEMPTING STOWAWAY

Captain Blackheart roves the seas. He steers clear of romantic entanglements that could tie him to land. Blackheart shouldn't have any trouble keeping his hands off the gently-bred lady he's commissioned to abduct. Except his cargo turns out to be feisty and passionate. She'd be a prize worth treasuring, if having her aboard didn't jeopardize everything...

Clara Halton thought the worst loss she could suffer was to be stripped of her family. Then she meets Blackheart. Their attraction is ruinous...and irresistible. When he delivers her to his client like so much plunder, his mission is over — but hers has just begun. She'll force him to acknowledge their connection, even if she must storm his ship to do it!

SNEAK PEEK

THE PIRATE'S TEMPTING STOWAWAY

February 1816
The Dark Crystal
Atlantic Ocean

The dread pirate Blackheart stood at the bow of his ship, smiling into the rush of salty air, as the first hint of America rose upon the horizon.

Despite the chill of winter, the skies were clear and blue, with both the wind and the sun to his back. 'Twas more than a good omen. It was a perfect day for any number of Captain Blackheart's favorite activities. Sailing. Wenching. Drinking. Horse-racing. Sword-fighting. Boarding enemy vessels. Commandeering an ill-fortuned frigate.

Nothing was better than the freedom of the seas.

"Land ho!" came the familiar cry from the crow's nest.

Blackheart's good humor faded. He relinquished navigational oversight to the Quartermaster without a word.

There was no need to bark orders. Most of the

crew had been part of his family long enough to recognize the storm clouds brewing in Blackheart's eyes, and every hand on board already had their standing orders.

No unnecessary fighting. No drinking to excess. Wenching was always permissible, but only if the crew made haste. The *Dark Crystal* would only be docked at the Port of Philadelphia long enough for Blackheart to accomplish his mission, and then they'd sail down the Delaware River and back out to sea just as swiftly as they'd sailed in.

Payment would only be delivered upon receipt of the booty. In this case...a sickly old woman named Mrs. Halton.

Despite being a pirate for hire, Blackheart was not in the habit of kidnapping innocents. Prior to the end of the war eight short months ago, he had been a privateer for the Royal Navy. A government pirate. A *legal* pirate. Now that he was an independent contractor, he tried to uphold the spirit (if not the precise letter) of the law.

'Twas the surest way to steer clear of the gallows.

The soles of Blackheart's boots tread silently against polished wood as he strode aft toward the gunroom skylight. He descended the ladder to the Captain's cabin and slipped inside to gather his supplies.

Item the first: a freshly starched cravat. This mission would require charm. Item the second: a freshly cleaned pistol and extra ammunition. A pirate might not *expect* trouble, but he certainly intended to finish it. Item the third: a heavy coin purse. If everything else failed, gold was often more powerful than bullets. And he planned on using every weapon at his disposal.

By the time the schooner docked at the port,

THE BRIGADIER'S RUNAWAY BRIDE

Blackheart was clean-shaven, dandified, and fresh as a daisy. Oh, certainly, his sun-bronzed skin was an unaristocratic brown—and was generously adorned with a truly ungentlemanly quantity of scars—but most of that was hidden away beneath his gleaming Hessians, soft buckskin breeches, muted chestnut waistcoat, blinding white cravat, and dark blue tailcoat with twin rows of gold buttons.

The hidden pistol in its fitted sling made barely a bulge beneath so many layers of foppery.

He forewent both sword and walking stick because he intended to make the rest of the journey on horseback, and debated leaving his hat behind as well. It was unlikely to stay on his head at a gallop, and would be crushed in the saddlebag...

With a sigh, Blackheart scooped up the beaver hat and shoved it on his head. He had no idea how easily manipulated Mrs. Halton might be, or whether she'd turn out to be one of those histrionic old matrons who refused to be seen in public alongside a gentleman with a bare head.

Plan B was to toss her over his shoulder and have done with the matter, but Blackheart had promised the Earl of Carlisle he'd at least *try* to coax the package into accompanying him voluntarily.

And although Blackheart would never admit it aloud, he had a rather high opinion of both his own charm *and* grandmotherly women. He would do everything within his power to make the journey to England a pleasant one for Mrs. Halton, and had already instructed his crew to treat her as if she were their own mother. With any luck, she'd be the sort to bake pies and biscuits. Or at least not to get seasick all over the *Dark Crystal*.

Carrying nothing more than a pair of gloves and a small satchel, he made his way down the gangplank in search of the fastest horse to rent—and nearly tripped over an underfed newspaper boy hawking today's headlines for a penny.

Under normal circumstances, Blackheart would have flipped the boy a coin and let him keep the paper...but the black font stamped across the top stopped the captain in his tracks.

MOST DANGEROUS PIRATE: THE CRIMSON CORSAIR

BLACKHEART SNATCHED up the paper and tried to read over the grinding of his teeth. He wasn't certain what he hated most about the Crimson Corsair: that the man was a dishonorable, coldblooded madman, or that he'd started to receive better press than Blackheart himself.

"You gonna pay for that, mister?" came a belligerent, high-pitched voice below his elbow.

He slapped the newspaper back onto the pile along with a shiny new coin, and stalked off the dock. Now was not the time to think about the Crimson Corsair. Once Mrs. Halton was safely delivered, Blackheart and his crew would be free to pursue any mission they wished—perhaps a quick seek-and-destroy of the corsair's vessel—but for the moment, he needed to stay focused. Not only had he given Carlisle his word, this mission would be a doddle. Grab the woman, get the money. The easiest three hundred pounds of his life.

The Pennsylvania countryside flew past, the sky darkening as he rode. Blackheart kept to the mail roads in order to trade for fresh horses at posting-houses…and also to keep from losing his way. He was used to England and to the open sea, not these sparsely populated American trails winding endlessly between bigger cities. He never felt comfortable when he was out of sight from the water, and he was heading further from the ocean with every step.

Despite the impressive number of small towns intersecting the long dusty roads, he felt more isolated with each passing mile. The hurried meals he took in country taverns were nothing like the rowdy camaraderie aboard his ship. He could scarcely wait to complete this mission.

Fortunately, he had to spend the night at an inn only once before finally reaching the town where his target resided.

The shabby little cottage was right where his instructions said it would be, but the state of disrepair gave Blackheart pause. The garden was so overgrown as to be nearly wild. The exterior was dirty and covered in spider webs. No smoke rose from the chimney. No candlelight shone in the windows.

Had someone already abducted his quarry? Had she simply moved? Or, God forbid, died of old age during his journey from England?

Rather than blindly march into unknown territory, he turned his horse in search of the local postmaster, in order to determine whether his target was still in his sights—or whether the rules of the game had changed.

"Mrs. Halton?" repeated the pale-faced postmaster when Blackheart interrupted his nuncheon. "Mrs. Clara Halton?"

"Yes," Blackheart replied calmly, as he towered over the dining table. "I've come to pay her a visit."

"But you mustn't, sir." The postmaster forged on

despite the captain's raised brow. "You cannot. She's ill—"

"I'm aware that Mrs. Halton has been sickly."

"—with consumption," the postmaster finished, his eyes wide with foreboding.

Although Blackheart's smile didn't falter, his blood ran cold. *Consumption*. The game had indeed changed.

"How long has she been afflicted?" he asked quietly.

"I don't rightly know—"

"How long does the doctor think she has?"

"I don't...He hasn't seen her since the diagnosis."

"Hasn't *seen* her?" Blackheart frowned. "She won't allow him in?"

"He hasn't gone." The postmaster's cheeks flushed. "It's the contagion, sir, can't you understand? He's the sole medical practitioner for miles, and if *he* catches the illness..."

The spider webs and overgrown garden now made perfect sense. Blackheart's jaw tightened. They'd left her to die. "If the sole medical practitioner does not visit his patient, I presume neither do the dairy maids or local farmers."

"No, sir. I can't even deliver her letters anymore. Too dangerous. We could die if we caught—"

"Without food or medicine, how is Mrs. Halton expected to live?"

"She *ain't* expected to live, sir. That's the point you keep missing. Most folks with consumption don't last longer than—"

"You said you possess post you've failed to deliver? Hand it over."

"You can't possibly intend to—"

"Now."

The postmaster scrambled up from the table and

hurried over to a cubicle, from which he drew two folded missives. "I wouldn't normally hand post to a stranger—"

"—but since you've no intention to deliver it anyway..." Blackheart finished dryly as he shoved the letters into his coat pocket. He turned toward the door, but then paused to pin the postmaster in his stare one final time. "Keep in mind, not everyone dies of consumption—but we all die of starvation."

He stalked back outside without waiting for a reply. There was nothing the postmaster could say that would be worth the time it took to listen. Perhaps Mrs. Halton's consumption was in fact fatal. Most afflicted parties did not survive more than a year or two after diagnosis.

But not all.

Blackheart should know.

He'd been eight years old when consumption had attacked his father. Then his mother. He'd still been young Gregory Steele in those days, and no lock in the house could keep him from his parents' sickbed for long.

What they'd thought was pneumonia had proven otherwise the moment they'd started coughing up blood. Then one of the nurses became infected. Another—just like little Gregory—developed a few of the symptoms, but eventually overcame the illness.

He was in perfect health the day they'd buried his parents in the ground.

His fingers clenched. Depending on Mrs. Halton's condition, he might not be able to complete this mission. But the least he could do was deliver the lady's mail.

He tied his horse to the rusting iron post at the edge of Mrs. Halton's overgrown front walk and rolled back his shoulders. For the next few minutes at least, he would not be Captain Blackheart, second-most feared pirate upon the high seas. Instead, he would be Mr. Gregory Steele. Again.

It had been so long since he'd last removed his mask, he'd nearly forgotten what being plain Mr. Steele felt like. It was so easy to forget that "Blackheart" was a persona and Gregory Steele was the real man. Especially when he liked being a pirate so much better.

He rapped his fingers against the door.

No one answered.

He glanced around for a knocker. There was none. He rapped harder. Thunder rumbled overhead.

No one answered.

His stomach twisted. He couldn't help but note the very Steele dismay at the idea of arriving too late to save a total stranger. A pirate like Blackheart would only care that he and his men had been effectively swindled by the earl who'd set them upon this impossible mission.

Gregory Steele, however, would deal with Carlisle and the crew later. First, he needed to determine whether his quarry was still alive—and figure out what to do next.

"Mrs. Halton?" he called, tramping across overgrown grass to squint through a grimy window. "Are you in there?"

"Go away!" returned a muffled female voice from the other side of the wall.

Steele's shoulders loosened. Relief rushed through him even though he well knew Mrs. Halton's non-dead state didn't mean any of their lives were about to get easier. One step at a time.

"Mrs. Halton, my name is Mr. Gregory Steele, and I have come all the way from London, England to—"

"Go *away*," the stubborn voice repeated. "I'm armed."

A grin played at the edges of Steele's lips. Pirate or not, he did love a good gunfight. Any old woman cantankerous enough to suggest one was well on her way to being a kindred spirit.

"I'm not here to rob you, ma'am. I—"

"Well, I'm not here to *kill* you. I've consumption, which is almost always fatal. I shan't be giving it to you."

Almost always. Steele's smile faded and he considered the closed door with renewed respect. If the occupant was aware of the minuscule chance that she might not die, she was also probably aware that temporary exposure to an invalid did not necessarily—or even usually—result in the infection of the caretaker. And yet Mrs. Halton still valued a stranger's life over any concern for her own.

"You're not going to shoot me," he said calmly.

"Try me."

Her voice didn't *sound* grandmotherly. But then, they were on opposite sides of a wall. He needed to put paid to this farce. She would realize soon enough that even real weapons were no deterrent. Her empty threats were laughable.

"If you wished for me to die, you'd have no objection to me entering a sick chamber."

"Perhaps I simply wish for you to die *quickly*," came the cheeky response.

He blinked and then bit back a silent laugh. How long had it been since last he'd been threatened to his face? Years. Not since becoming Blackheart. No one had dared to challenge him. Until today.

"Please open the door. I'm coming inside."

"I'm busy adding extra powder to my pistol to

make certain the first ball takes you down if you come near my door."

"Most pistols only *have* one ball, Mrs. Halton. If you miss, you won't even have time to reload it. Besides, we both know you haven't—" Steele paused at the familiar sound of a ramrod forcing a patched ball down a metallic chamber. "You have a *pistol?*"

"You really should consider leaving before I've finished loading it. Oh, bother...I've finished. A smart man would take his leave."

Steele stepped away from the window in case the dear old bat was mad enough to shoot him.

He ran his hands down his coat. He, too, had a pistol. And, no, he would not be drawing it. He had something even more powerful.

Letters.

"Stopped by the postmaster on my way to your cottage," he said conversationally. "Seems to have forgotten to drop off a couple of items. First letter is from a..." He squinted at the spidery script. "Can't rightly say. 'Mayer,' perhaps?"

"My father?" The voice on the other side of the wall sounded tiny and shocked. "What does it say?"

"The second one was franked by the Earl of Carlisle but seems to be from a Miss Grace Halton. Relation of yours, is it?"

"My daughter," Mrs. Halton breathed, her voice so quiet and so close that Steele could imagine her pressing up against the wall to be closer to the letter. "Read it to me."

He shoved them back into his coat pocket as noisily as possible. "Let me in, and I will."

"Blackguard," she hissed.

He smiled. "You have no idea."

Silence reigned for a scant moment before the

soft sound of a tumbler indicated the front lock had been disengaged.

The door did not swing open.

Steele strode up and let himself in, just as the first drops of rain began to fall from the sky.

The tiny cottage consisted of very few rooms—all of which were visible from the vantage point of the front door. No candles were lit and no fire burned in the grate, but enough natural light filtered in through the windows to illuminate the musty, but surprisingly clean interior.

The furnishings were shabby and worn, but otherwise spotless. The dishes were clean. The beds were made. The woman aiming a triple-barrel flintlock turnover pistol toward Steele's midsection was bathed and neat.

And not a day older than Steele himself.

Where his own beard was starting to appear more salt and pepper these days, Mrs. Halton's long black hair cascaded down her back with nary a hint of gray. Dark eyelashes framed wide green eyes. He swallowed and tried not to stare. She was beautiful. Porcelain skin. Rosy lips.

The lady didn't look sick. She didn't even look like the right person.

He narrowed his eyes. "How can you possibly be the mother of a grown woman? Or…acquainted with the Earl of Carlisle?"

"Read me the letter, and perhaps we'll both find out." She gestured at him with the pistol. "Better yet, leave my correspondence on the table, and see your way out."

"Why don't you put that thing down before you lose a hand? Multi-cylinder pistols have been known to explode rather than eject their ammunition. Yours looks like it's twenty years old."

"It is. I bought it after my husband was killed and taught myself to shoot it. Don't worry, it won't misfire. I clean it every night."

The increase in Steele's heart rate had nothing to do with fear and everything to do with the confident woman in front of him. Owning a gun had made her interesting to him. Being willing to use it had made her even more so. Now that he saw it for himself and realized not only was it three-barreled firepower instead of a lady's simple muff pistol, but that she also knew how to take care of it…and herself… He was very, very interested.

He held out his palm. "Give me the gun."

"Why would I do so, when I've the upper hand?" She succeeded quite admirably with sending an imperious glare down her nose until a sudden violent cough wracked her thin shoulders. She hid her face behind her elbow until the onslaught passed.

Steele backed up a step without even realizing it, unable to tamp a frisson of remembered terror from sliding down his spine. As soon as she was done coughing, he stepped forward and lowered his voice. "Give me the pistol now, or I'll wait until your next coughing fit and take it from you."

Green eyes flashing in silent fury, she slid the flint out of the pistol's jaws and slapped the disarmed weapon into his upturned hand. "Give me the letters."

"In a moment." He helped himself to the larger of two uncomfortable-looking chairs. "How long have you had consumption?"

"I started coughing about six months ago." She sank into the chair opposite him as if she no longer had the ability to stand.

He couldn't help but remember watching his parents' eventual decline into death. How angry he had felt. How helpless. But at least they hadn't been alone.

He softened his voice. "How did you know it was consumption?"

"A traveling surgeon told me in November. There had been other cases nearby, and when he learned I'd been sick for three months... He just knew."

Steele frowned. "He knew, or he examined you?"

"Of course he examined me. From a safe distance. I was already bedridden. Even now, I can't keep my feet for more than a quarter hour at a time without losing my breath. Once he told me he suspected consumption, I sent my daughter as far away as I could. May I please read her letter?"

"In a moment." He held up a finger at her glare. "I'm not being cruel. We both know you'll stop listening to me the moment I hand over the post. I'm trying to understand the timing. When your daughter left, she didn't know your diagnosis?"

Mrs. Halton shook her head. "If I'd told her, she would never have left. And I couldn't have her death on my conscience."

"How did you get her to leave? Triple-barrel turnover pistol, I presume?"

She smiled sadly. "I lied. Oldest trick there is. I told her there was a miracle cure we didn't have enough money for, and that if she went to England to find her grandparents, perhaps they would give the money to her. If not outright, then as a dowry."

"And you've been wasting away ever since? How are you managing, with no servants and no food?"

"I have a patch of vegetables behind the cottage, between the fruit trees. It takes me all day to tend what a farmer might in a mere hour, but I've nothing else to do with my time, other than wait to die. And count the raindrops every time the roof leaks."

A vegetable garden. Steele tilted his head to consider her. She was clearly exhausted, clearly *ill*—those wet, wracking coughs could not be faked—and yet, to his eye, she didn't remotely look like she was dying. Pneumonia, he could perhaps believe. On the other hand, she'd been sick for half a year already. And a surgeon had made the diagnosis.

A traveling surgeon, Steele reminded himself. A traveling surgeon who had examined his patient from a safe distance across the room. Which likely meant he hadn't examined her at all.

"When did the blood start?"

She crossed her legs. "The what?"

"Coughing up blood." Steele's parents' eyes had gone bloodshot and puffy around the same time the blood began, and had never recovered. Once they'd become bedridden, they hadn't left their sickroom again. "Have you been coughing up blood since November?"

Her forehead creased. "No."

"When did it start?"

"It hasn't. Yet. I've all the other symptoms—fatigue, cough, chest pain, chills, weight loss. It's just a matter of time."

Steele stared at her, then leapt out of the chair. He did his best thinking on his feet and he needed to come up with something. Perhaps it wasn't just a matter of time. Perhaps there was hope.

Her eyes widened. "What are you doing?"

"Reconnaissance." He tossed the letters into her lap and began to pace the small cottage. Was it possible? Might she not have consumption after all? Or was it wishful thinking from a man who couldn't bear to watch anyone else die from such a disease?

He was no doctor. Prior to turning to a life at sea, Steele had been a barrister. But success in both law and piracy required an observant eye, an infallible memory, and an analytical mind. One did not present one's case unless one could predict every word and every reaction from both the judge and the witnesses. Likewise, one did not board an enemy ship without knowing exactly who was on board and what, precisely, awaited them.

This, however, was a special case.

First evidence: no blood. Granted, this was usually a later sign—once all hope truly was gone—but six months had gone by and Mrs. Halton's cough was no worse than someone with pneumonia or lesser illnesses.

Second evidence: Mrs. Halton was still alive. If the servants had abandoned Steele's parents as they lay upon their sickbed, they would have died from lack of food and water. In contrast, Mrs. Halton tended a garden. Slowly, perhaps. A tiny one, yes. But she withstood the sun and she cooked her own meals and she tidied after herself. None of which was typical behavior for an invalid dying of consumption.

Third evidence: Her symptoms. Weight loss? See: tiny garden, and forced to cook her own meals. Night chills? It was February. She had no fire. Fatigue, cough, chest pain? Pneumonia. Influenza. Asthma. Whooping cough. Any number of diseases that were uncomfortable or even dangerous, yet not life-threatening. But how could he be certain?

He couldn't.

His fingers curled into fists. He hated to leave her behind. What if she worsened? She couldn't count on any of her neighbors dropping by with milk or broth.

On the other hand, what if the surgeon was right? What if he brought her aboard the ship only for her to start spitting up blood and infecting his entire crew while they floated in the middle of the ocean?

Lightning flashed outside the south windows.

Mrs. Halton dragged herself up off her chair and

to the kitchen, where she gathered a collection of pots and pans and began to position them strategically throughout the cottage.

Steele blinked. "What the devil are you doing, woman?"

She pointed overhead. "Rotted ceiling, remember?"

He tilted his gaze upward and took an involuntary step back. So much for his infallible memory. She was right—the ceiling leaked. What she had failed to mention was that the rotting roof was coated in slimy mold. Flecks of the dark fungus dripped down with the rain to splat in the thick iron pans. The rest clung to the ceiling, growing outward from the wet areas until fingers of furry mold brushed against the tops of the walls like a living black carpet.

The back of Steele's throat tickled just from looking at all that mold. They were *breathing* it right now.

"Pack a bag," he barked as he ducked into her bedchamber to start throwing open drawers.

She glanced up from arranging the pots, startled. "What? Why?"

"You're coming with me."

"But I have—"

"I don't think you do." He threw a large cloth bag onto the bed. "Pack it."

"You may be used to getting your way due to your looks and your arrogance, but I'm not willing to risk other people's lives based on what you think."

"You won't be risking everyone's lives. Just mine." He tossed a pair of stockings into the open bag. "You'll be quarantined with me."

ABOUT THE AUTHOR

Erica Ridley is a *New York Times* and *USA Today* bestselling author of witty, feel-good historical romance novels, including THE DUKE HEIST, featuring the Wild Wynchesters. Why seduce a duke the normal way, when you can accidentally kidnap one in an elaborately planned heist?

In the *12 Dukes of Christmas* series, enjoy witty, heartwarming Regency romps nestled in a picturesque snow-covered village. After all, nothing heats up a winter night quite like finding oneself in the arms of a duke!

Two popular series, the *Dukes of War* and *Rogues to Riches*, feature roguish peers and dashing war heroes who find love amongst the splendor and madness of Regency England.

When not reading or writing romances, Erica can be found eating couscous in Morocco, zip-lining through rainforests in Central America, or getting hopelessly lost in the middle of Budapest.

∾

Let's be friends! Find Erica on:
www.EricaRidley.com

Printed in Great Britain
by Amazon